APACHE RAID

Reaching the wagon, White Apache ducked under it as three soldiers on foot appeared on the run and blasted away. Their shots chipped off slivers of wood. White Apache rolled to the right, came out from under the wagon, and dashed to the rear. He knew they would look underneath and spot his legs, so he swiftly climbed onto the wheel, using the spokes as steps, high enough so they couldn't see him.

Perched on the wheel, White Apache transferred the Winchester to his left hand and drew a Colt. No sooner had he done so than one of the foot soldiers barreled around the tail end of the wagon, his rifle leveled at waist height. Too late, the man saw White Apache. A bullet through the right eye flattened him where he stood.

Someone cursed on the other side. White Apache twisted. Another soldier was coming around in front of the team of oxen. He, too, was looking low when he should have been looking higher up. White Apache banged off two shots. The soldier jerked to the impact, staggered, and keeled over.

D1410025

7

WHITE APACHE

BLOOD BOUNTY

Jake McMasters

LEISURE BOOKS   NEW YORK CITY

To Judy, Joshua, and Shane.

A LEISURE BOOK®

May 1995

Published by

Dorchester Publishing Co., Inc.
276 Fifth Avenue
New York, NY 10001

Chapter One

The wagon train wound slowly northward across the bleak, dry landscape. Capt. Gonzalo Cruz took a handkerchief from his shirt pocket, squinted up at the blazing sun, and mopped his sweating brow. It was summer in the state of Chihuahua, the heat almost unbearable, but the hot weather was the least of the captain's worries.

Neatly folding the handkerchief, he placed it back in his pocket and took his spyglass from its case, which hung by a strap from his saddle horn. The small telescope had cost him three month's salary, but it was worth every peso in his estimation. It had saved his life more than once.

Capt. Cruz surveyed the countryside. To the northeast were low hills, to the west a vast wasteland no one penetrated. Not Mexicans, at any rate. He saw lizards and snakes and several hardy sparrows, but not that which he dreaded.

There was no sign of Apaches, yet.

The captain shifted in the saddle to solemnly regard the wagon train plodding along in his wake. Twenty wagons, all heavily laden, were bound for Janos. His orders were to escort the train and keep the people safe, a formidable task with but fifteen soldiers assigned to the patrol and only four of them mounted. But that had been all the colonel could spare, what with the shortages of men and horseflesh on the frontier. So Cruz had squared his shoulders and told his superior not to worry, that he would see the wagons reached Janos without mishap.

A brazen statement, the captain now reflected, words which might come back to haunt him later for no one ever knew when and where the notorious Apaches might strike. They were like ghosts, able to flit about from place to place with a speed no ordinary man could match. One day they would raid a small village at the base of the Sierra Madres, and the next day the very same band would strike up near Ciudad Juarez.

The poor farmers and town dwellers, who were often victims, lived in perpetual fear of the savage marauders. Many believed Apaches were not human. Cruz had once heard the mayor of a remote village, a respected and sane man, claim that Apaches were demons in mortal guise.

Captain Cruz knew better. Apaches were flesh and blood. They could be killed like other men. When they were shot or stabbed, they bled.

Three years ago he had been a lowly lieutenant on patrol near the American border. He had risen early and made for the brush to heed nature's call. In the process he had stumbled on a warrior trying to steal a horse from the string.

It had been hard to say which of them had been the

more surprised. The Apache had turned to flee and been thwarted when the horse stepped in front of him. Cruz had fumbled at his holster and somehow produced his pistol. He had fired without thinking, acting on sheer instinct, spurred by raw fear. And he had shot the Apache squarely in the back.

Much had been made of the deed. Cruz had received a commendation in front of the entire garrison. He was sure that killing the warrior had earned him the rank of captain much sooner than he would have been promoted otherwise.

For weeks afterward, Cruz had not had to buy a single drink with his own money. He was the talk of the post. The Apache Killer, the men dubbed him, and the nickname stuck.

It did not seem to matter to anyone else that the Apache had been a mere boy, or that Cruz had accidentally shot the youth in the back. All that mattered was the fact there was one less demon in the world.

Cruz had tried to shut that awful event from his mind but he often relived it in his sleep and would wake up in a cold sweat. He would see the Apache's twitching body, see the blood gushing from the wound and soaking the ground. He knew that he should not let it get to him but he could not help himself.

In his own eyes, Cruz had done a cowardly thing. In the eyes of everyone else, he was a hero.

Life was so strange sometimes.

The thud of hooves shattered the officer's reflective mood and he glanced at the stocky soldier approaching. "What is it, Sergeant Hernandez?" he demanded. "I gave you clear orders to stay at the rear of the train and goad on stragglers."

"Yes, Captain," the noncom said stiffly, "but I thought you should know. Old Barrera claims he saw an Apache pacing us to the west."

Cruz sighed. "Farmers see Apaches in every shadow." Nonetheless, he raised the spyglass to his right eye and scanned the arid flatland. There was brush and cactus and a few small boulders but no evidence of a lurking warrior. "Was he sipping tequila when he made the claim?"

"No, sir. Barrera has not touched a drop since we left the post. He says he wants to have a clear head so he can run faster when the Apaches attack."

"Tell him to quit scaring the women and children," Cruz ordered. "And remind everyone that we are only two days from Janos. Soon they can all stop worrying."

"Yes, sir."

The captain replaced the precious spyglass, then jabbed his heels into the flanks of his sorrel. He had to hold the animal to a slow walk or he would soon outdistance the wagon train, which wound along with all the speed of a decrepit tortoise. The oxen hung their heads, the mules were little better off. Many drivers dozed in their seats, their faces screened by sombreros.

The sun passed its zenith and arched toward the far horizon. Shimmering waves of heat rippled on all sides, distorting objects at a distance. Once Cruz could have sworn he saw a lake where he knew there was none.

From time to time the captain made it a point to study the wasteland, just in case. Other than a solitary hawk wheeling high on the air currents, nothing moved. He was convinced that old man Barrera had let his imagination get the better of him. There were no Apaches out there.

* * *

But Capt. Gonzalo Cruz was wrong.

Unknown to him, five pairs of eyes intently observed the lumbering progress of the wagon train. Four pair were quite similar, dark eyes framed by the bronzed features of Chiricahua warriors. The fifth pair was unique. Lake-blue eyes framed by a face equally as bronzed, but definitely that of a white man, were fixed on the officer in charge.

To some men north of the border, the owner of those striking blue eyes had once been known as Clay Taggart, resident of Arizona Territory, mildly prosperous rancher.

Now everyone in the Southwest and in Mexico knew him by another name. To the Americans, he was the feared White Apache, a renegade who had launched a killing spree unrivaled in Arizona history. To the Mexicans he was the White Apache, the demon of demons, a bloodthirsty wraith the army was unable or unwilling to bring to bay.

For months the White Apache had been leading his Chiricahua brothers on raid after raid. They had fought off the American Fifth Cavalry, they had beaten federales. Lawmen were powerless against them. Just the mention of his name was enough to frighten children in remote villages.

He was a fiend.

He was a butcher.

He was the devil.

The White Apache knew of the tales told about him and laughed at the stupidity of the sheep he sheared. At this particular moment, he was intent on shearing some more. For two days his band had shadowed the train, noting the number of soldiers and men with rifles, noting which wagons contained women and which did not.

It was safe to say that the Apaches knew the daily routine of the travelers as well as the travelers themselves.

Early that morning White Apache and three of the four Chiricahuas with him had gone on ahead of the wagon train to conceal themselves. In an area bordering the rutted tracks which clearly marked the Janos road, they had dug shallow holes large enough for them to lie in on their backs. Then they had covered themselves with loose dirt and broken bits of brush collected for that purpose. By the time they were done, no one other than another Apache could have told they were there.

One of their number paced the wagons to be sure there were no nasty surprises. Ponce was his name, the youngest of the renegade band, a muscular warrior who aspired to one day be a great leader like Cochise and Mangus Coloradas. It was Ponce whom old man Barrera had glimpsed as the Chiricahua slipped from one barrel cactus to another.

If Ponce had known, he would have been ashamed of himself for being so careless. Stealth was as important to an Apache as the two main virtues of being able to steal without being caught and killing without being killed.

Truth to tell, the inexperienced Ponce was upset, which explained why he had been careless. His mind was too much occupied with White Apache's plan when he should have been paying attention to the things around him.

From behind a clump of brush no bigger than a basket, Ponce admired a particular female of the Nakaiyes, a shapely young beauty who sat perched on a wagon, her long raven tresses fanned by the sluggish breeze. Ponce looked, and hungered.

Almost too late, the warrior remembered White Apache's instructions. When the train reached a certain point, he was to race ahead. Already the first few wagons had passed the curve.

Ponce tore his gaze from the woman and flew northward, using every lick of cover to its best advantage, snaking along the ground where there was none. Always he was careful not to raise puffs of dust or let the sun glint off his Winchester or the pistol he wore.

Outpacing the wagons was so easy a child could have done it. Ponce came to the spot White Apache had selected and saw where the four men were hidden. But he could not tell who was whom.

"Lickoyee-shis-inday?" Ponce whispered.

A layer of dirt stirred and White Apache sat up. His sinews rippled as he moved, while his long hair swirled when he gave a toss of his head to cast off dust. Other than those eyes of his, he was like an Apache in every respect. "They come at last?"

"Yes. Do you want me to go on watching them?" Ponce asked a bit too eagerly. Secretly, he yearned to feast his eyes on the vision of loveliness who had caught his fancy.

White Apache suppressed a grin. It was plain the young warrior was excited, and he couldn't blame him. But he also knew that warriors who let their thoughts stray when on a raid often paid for their lapses with their lives. "Join us. Hurry."

A nearby section of earth shifted and a gruff voice declared, "What is the hurry, Lickoyee-shis-inday? A dead man can move faster than the Nakai-yes. It must be true that their race was bred from snails."

The speaker was Fiero, biggest and surliest of all the warriors, a firebrand aptly named. In battle there were none braver. He was renowned within the tribe as their best fighter, but so fierce was he that the Chiricahuas themselves fought shy of him. Quick to take insult, quicker to retaliate, his temper had always been his glaring weakness.

At that moment Fiero was as upset as Ponce, but for a different reason. He disliked laying low when there was no need. In his view, Mexicans were curs, hardly worth the effort it took to kill them. "The Nakai-yes do not count as men," he liked to say. "We can kill them with rocks."

And when other warriors would point out that many Mexicans were brave and recounted times when the Mexicans had held their own, Fiero would laugh them to scorn. He knew better, having slain dozens.

So White Apache was not surprised by the comment. Settling back down and covering himself again, he listened to the raspy grate of Ponce digging. His right hand closed on the rifle at his side and he slowed his breathing, resigning himself to a long wait.

Once, such patience had been alien to Clay Taggart's nature. But since taking up with the Chiricahuas, he had learned many new ways and found strengths he had never known he had. Patience was just one of them.

White Apache had also developed an endurance few white man could boast of. Like his Apache brothers, he was able to run for hours on end, at times covering 70 miles at a stretch without so much as a sip of water. He could climb as agilely as a bighorn. And the broiling sun no longer bothered him as it once had.

Should any of his old pards see him, Taggart was sure none would recognize their drinking companion. Not only was his skin as dark as burnt toast and his hair five times as long, his formerly weak muscles were corded like bands of iron. From a distance he could pass for a genuine Apache, which he considered flattering.

At length the digging stopped. White Apache thought of the other two warriors, Delgadito and Cuchillo Negro, and wondered how they felt about his scheme. Neither had uttered a word when he first told them about it, which was not at all unusual. Apaches were laconic by nature, more so when they were upset. They kept their hurts and disappointments inside themselves. While Clay did not always agree with their outlook, he did respect it.

Suddenly, White Apache noticed movement at ground level out of the corner of his right eye. He shifted his eyeballs, not his head, thinking it might be a lizard or a bird. It was a large scorpion.

He held himself rigid as the creature shuffled toward him with its tail curled above its back and its pincers held as if ready to rend and tear. Usually, scorpions came out to hunt at night. Only when they were very hungry did they venture abroad during the day.

This one was a giant desert hairy scorpion. Its nasty pincers, scuttling legs, and poised tail were all pale yellow, while its abdomen was black.

White Apache watched as the terror of the desert came closer and closer to his face. Enough dust covered him that he barely felt its legs until it reached his right shoulder. Here, he must have left a bare spot because suddenly his skin pricked as if a dozen needles had been jabbed into him at once. Gritting his teeth, he stayed as still as a log, knowing that if he so much as flinched the scorpion might sense an enemy and strike.

The creature came nearer still, almost to his cheek. White Apache tried not to think of what would happen if the thing stung him in the eye. He saw it wave its pincers in the air, then turn its hind end toward him. The stinger lowered. For a few tense moments he dreaded the scorpion would lash out. But the little monster harmlessly swung its tail a few times and faced him again.

The scorpion moved onto White Apache's face, so close to his partially buried nose that he held his breath to keep from disturbing it. He had to swivel his eyes as low as they would go to see the thing.

Tense moments went by. White Apache wanted the creature to go on about its business but it seemed to be content where it was. Suddenly he lost sight of it, and the next moment he felt its legs on his lips. Once more the living nightmare stopped.

White Apache didn't twitch a muscle. He waited for the scorpion to move on. But to his dismay, it stayed there. His lungs started to ache so he slowly emptied them through his nose. A few more seconds, and relief flooded through him as the thing walked on. Oddly, though, it only appeared to be shifting position. He couldn't understand why until something nipped at his lower lip, then at his upper one.

It took all of five seconds for the awful truth to register. White Apache realized the scorpion was trying to pry his mouth open with its pincers. Possibly it was drawn to the heat given off by his body. Or maybe it sensed a cavity of some sort. Scorpions loved to crawl into holes.

White Apache clamped his lips shut and grit his teeth. The pincers prodded and poked, exploring. He swore the thing could tell the difference between his mouth and the surrounding skin because it concentrated strictly on the crack between his lips.

His nerves were strained to their limit, and beyond. Having to lie there helpless while the creature pried and pinched was almost more than he could endure. His skin crawled when his lower lip was squeezed so hard, it split.

Abruptly, the scorpion stopped moving. White Apache could just make out the top of its tail, held motionless above his mouth. Soon there was a new sensation, and for the life of him he couldn't make sense of it. Something was picking at a spot on his lip, lightly touching it again and again, but it did not feel like a pincer or leg. Only when a slick drop trickled down his chin did he figure out that the scorpion was evidently tasting his blood.

There were limits even to his self-control. He was about to leap up and swat the creature off when a gleaming knife materialized above him, the long black hilt clasped in a sinewy hand. The blade flashed once and reappeared with the thrashing scorpion impaled.

The grinning face of Cuchillo Negro joined the knife. The warrior calmly regarded the creature a moment, then looked down. "I know that white-eyes are fond of keeping pets, as you call them, but I would suggest you find another." The face vanished.

White Apache raised up high enough to see the warrior lowering himself into the ground. Of all the Chiricahuas, he had grown fondest of Black Knife, as the warrior was known to the Mexicans.

Cuchillo Negro always treated White Apache as an equal. He never criticized, as Fiero was wont to do. He never badgered White Apache with questions, which Ponce sometimes did. Nor did Cuchillo Negro try to manipulate him as Delgadito had tried several times.

White Apache smiled in gratitude, which Cuchillo Negro acknowledged with a nod, and laid back down. He had been so distracted by the scorpion that he was shocked to hear the creak of saddle leather and the rattle of wagons wheels. They were very close. It would soon be time.

The buzz of many people speaking in low voices filled the stifling air. Clay Taggart knew Spanish well enough to hold his own in day to day palaver. He heard a man talking about the recent lack of rain, heard another lament the long trip to Janos. A woman was singing softly, a love song about a vaquero who romanced a maiden, went to a cantina, and died in a gunfight.

White Apache firmed his grip on the Winchester. It was a new model, taken off a prospector he had slain in the Dragoons who must have ordered it from the factory back East within the past few months.

The barrel was only 24 inches long, which made it easy to carry over long distances, and since the caliber was .44-40, it had enough stopping power to drop a man or a bull buffalo. Not only that, White Apache could use the same cartridges the rifle took in his two Colt pistols, which spared him the petty nuisance of having to tote two heavy cartridge belts all over creation.

A horse nickered. Then a mule brayed.

White Apache debated whether the animals had caught their scent and decided against it. He had picked a spot due east of the road; the wind was blowing from the west.

Moments later a rider came into view, the officer in charge of the soldiers serving as escorts. The insignia on the man's uniform indicated he was a captain. The previous night, while concealed within a stone's throw of the camp, White Apache had overheard a passenger calling the man by his given name, Cruz.

Now Capt. Cruz raised a hand and drew rein. White

Apache guessed that the officer suspected something was amiss.

Which the captain did. His intuition screamed a silent warning in his brain, yet try as he might, Cruz was unable to pinpoint the reason. The wagon train was in the middle of flat, open country. No brush grew within 100 yards of where he was, nor were there any boulders nearby. Why then, he asked himself, did he feel as if unseen eyes were on him? Minutes elapsed but he saw nothing out of the ordinary.

Cpl. Jacquez trotted up and saluted. It was no secret that he was eager to be promoted to sergeant, which explained why he constantly brushed off his shirt and hat to present a neat appearance, as he did at this moment while asking, "Is anything wrong, Captain? The people in the wagons are worried."

Cruz glanced over a shoulder. Sure enough, many members of the train were staring at him in scarcely disguised fear. He knew what was uppermost on their minds: Apaches. "Spread the word that all is well. I had some dust in my eye, is all."

"Yes, sir." Cpl. Jacquez saluted sharply before riding off.

Capt. Cruz smiled. The man was so obvious, it was ridiculous. The rumor was that Jacquez wanted to marry a pretty senorita, but that her father forbid their union unless Jacquez climbed a grade in rank. A couple could not live on a corporal's pay, the father claimed, and Capt. Cruz had to agree. It was hard enough making ends meet on his income.

Shifting, the officer motioned for the wagons to forge on. He goaded his mount, which unexpectedly shied from the edge of the road. Fearing it had seen a rattler, he glanced down. Rattlesnakes liked to come out during the hottest part of the day to sun themselves. But there was no snake.

Capt. Cruz started to raise his head and froze. Peering back up at him from under the very ground were two of the bluest eyes he had ever seen. For a few seconds he thought that his imagination was playing tricks on him.

Then the earth erupted, spewing demons.

Chapter Two

Clay Taggart, the White Apache, was all too familiar with the fickle working of fate. If things could go wrong, they usually did. That old saw about the best laid plans of mice and men was as true during his time as it had been ages ago.

So when he saw the officer's horse shy and the man glance toward him, he was prepared. They locked eyes. The captain's amazement riveted him in place for several moments, all the time White Apache needed.

Venting a whoop, White Apache burst from concealment. He was so close to the officer's mount that he didn't bother to take aim and fire. He simply whipped the stock in a vicious arc and caught Capt. Cruz on the side of the head. The man crashed down without uttering a sound.

Simultaneously, the Chiricahuas, howling like mad, sprang from their holes and promptly spread out, bounding toward the wagons. The uproar they made was not meant to bolster their courage, as men often did in combat, since none of them knew the meaning of fear. No, they howled because they had learned that the more noise they made, the more fear they instilled in the hearts of the Nakai-yes. As they charged, they opened fire.

Whirling, White Apache tucked the stock of the .44-40 to his shoulder. Fifty feet away a corporal had turned his horse and sat gaping at the onrushing warriors. The man had a rifle which he tried to unlimber. White Apache cored his head with a well-placed slug.

Shrieking like a demented banshee, White Apache raced toward the lead wagon. A stout farmer had produced an antiquated flintlock and was fumbling with the stubborn hammer. Beside the man, an elderly woman cowered against the seat. White Apache shot the man dead. When the woman marshaled her courage and scooped up her husband's fallen rifle, White Apache shot her.

Once, months ago, Clay Taggart would have been horrified by his own actions. That was before his wealthy neighbor had stolen the heart of the woman he loved and trumped up lies about him in order to steal his land. That was before he had been saved from a lynching by Delgadito's band and the Chiricahuas had taken him under their wing. And that was before a bounty had been put on his head and every white man in Arizona had turned against him.

Now Clay Taggart considered himself more Apache than white, and to an Apache, every person not an Apache was an enemy to be killed as the need arose.

Reaching the wagon, White Apache ducked under it as three soldiers on foot appeared on the run and blasted away. Their shots chipped off slivers of wood. White Apache rolled to the right, came out from under

the wagon, and dashed to the rear. He knew they
would look underneath and spot his legs, so he swiftly
climbed onto the wheel, using the spokes as steps,
high enough so they couldn't see him.

Everywhere, guns boomed. Women were screaming, children wailing. Horses whinnied in panic.
Mules brayed wildly. Some of the wagon drivers were
desperately trying to turn their wagons around but in
all the confusion, they were making little headway.

Perched on the wheel, White Apache transferred the
Winchester to his left hand and drew a Colt. No
sooner had he done so than one of the foot soldiers
barreled around the tail end of the wagon, his rifle
leveled at waist height. Too late, the man saw White
Apache. A bullet through the right eye flattened him
where he stood.

Someone cursed on the other side. White Apache
twisted. Another soldier was coming around in front
of the team of oxen. He, too, was looking low when
he should have been looking higher up. White Apache
banged off two shots. The soldier jerked to the impact,
staggered, and keeled over. Which left one to deal
with.

Taking a gamble, White Apache leaped down, dropping into a crouch as he landed. The third soldier was
in the act of scooting under the wagon and was bent
over at the waist. The man opened his mouth to cry
out. With unerring skill, White Apache planted a slug
in the dark oval framed by the man's cavity-laced
teeth.

Darting to the next wagon, White Apache vaulted
onto the seat where a man already lay dead. Inside,
two young women cowered. One brandished a
butcher knife. White Apache raised the pistol as if to
shoot, and when the younger of the pair screeched, he

laughed and jumped back to the ground. They would keep until later, he reflected.

The battle was proving to be short-lived. In the short span since the clash began, the Chiricahuas had dispatched nine of the fifteen soldiers. The rest were slowly retreating along the line of wagons, firing as they backed up. A few members of the wagon train had joined them, but most of the pilgrims cowered in their wagons, too terrified to so much as peek out.

White Apache hurtled over the convulsing body of a man in a straw sombrero and ran to enter the fray.

The warriors were on both sides of the train, Fiero and Ponce to the east, Delgadito and Cuchillo Negro to the west. By staying low, darting from cover to cover and making every shot count, they slowly advanced. Never once did they recklessly expose themselves. It wasn't the Chiricahua way. Warriors who took needless risks were regarded as fools.

Dropping to his knees behind a bush, White Apache fixed a bead on a thin man in the clothes of a clerk who was firing a pistol. He held his breath to steady his aim, then lightly touched the trigger. The .44-40 boomed and bucked. At the retort, the clerk reacted as if kicked in the chest by one of the mules. The man slid a few feet when he was hit and went limp.

By this time the soldiers were close to the last wagon.

Six travelers, five of them men, were in full flight to the south, fleeing along the road with a speed born of stark fear.

White Apache glided to the right, behind a cactus. He trained the Winchester on a soldier but the man ducked from sight.

Moments later the soldiers reached the last wagon and stopped. One of their number appeared to be goading on the rest, rousing them to make a stand.

It was then that Fiero leaped forward like a tawny mountain lion closing in for the kill. He wasn't being reckless; he was being Fiero. Seized by blood lust, his scarred face contorted in feral glee, he zigzagged to make himself hard to hit while firing on the fly.

A shot clipped the soldier doing the goading. Another man caught him before he fell.

Fiero roared a challenge, never slowing his pace. It had always been this way with him. Since childhood he had reveled in war. At the age of nine he had slain his first enemy, a Mexican miner, by stabbing the man over and over. It had sent such a thrill coursing through him that even after the man lay dead, he had stabbed and stabbed and stabbed. To kill without being killed was more than Fiero's unwritten creed, to him it was life itself.

Unnerved, the soldiers broke and fled, firing at random, more intent on preserving their lives than on being accurate. They had done all they could do. To stay invited death.

White Apache rose. He knew that there was no use in calling Fiero back. He would be ignored. The warrior would chase the soldiers until they were either all dead or beyond reach.

Beckoning Ponce, White Apache indicated the wagons and directed in the Chiricahua tongue, "Go to each one. Round up the Nakai-yes."

Cuchillo Negro and Delgadito came running from the other side. Black Knife clambered onto a seat and disappeared in a wagon. Inside, a woman shrieked. From other wagons wafted the cries and blubbering of those too scared to resist or run.

Delgadito, wearing a rare smile, walked up to White Apache. Speaking in a mix of English and Chiricahua, he said, "Once again, nejeunee, your plan will bring us much reward. Truly, Lickoyee-shis-inday, your thoughts are as deep as the great canyon. You have learned much from us, but I never thought you would learn na-tse-kes so well."

Clay Taggart merely grunted. It was Delgadito who had saved him from the hangman's knot and he owed the warrior more than he could ever repay. But recently he had learned from Cuchillo Negro that Delgadito had been using him as a pawn all along. He hadn't figured out exactly how yet, but he knew enough to make him suspicious of anything the warrior said or did.

Not all that long ago Delgadito had been a respected Chiricahua leader with his own large band. When Cochise made a deal with the whites to set up the Chiricahua Reservation, he had grumbled but gone along with the tribal chief, who died shortly thereafter.

A new chief, Palacio, had taken Cochise's place, but Palacio had neither Cochise's prowess in war nor his eloquence at council. As a result, Palacio could not stop the spread of discontent.

Delgadito had decided reservation life was for dogs. Of most concern was the fact the whites would not let the warriors go on any raids. They demanded that the Chiricahuas not go beyond the confines of the reservation, under threat of punishment. Worse, the whites brought in many soldiers to make sure the Chiricahuas obeyed.

Then came the final insult. The Indian Agent in charge let it be known that the Great Father who lived far off in a place called Wash-een-tun wanted the Chiricahuas to take up tilling the soil like the lowly Pimas and Maricopas. Warriors were expected to cut their hair, to adopt white ways, and to send their children to the reservation school to learn to be white.

It had been too much to bear.

Gathering many warriors who felt as he did, Delgadito had fled the reservation with their women and children along. His idea had been to go deep into Mexico and live unmolested in the Sierra Madres. But they had been cut off and driven back by a vile band of scalphunters hired by the state of Sonora to exterminate Apaches.

Delgadito had retreated north of the border and made camp in a hollow, thinking he was safe. He knew that Mexican soldiers were not allowed to cross into Arizona and that American soldiers were not permitted to stray into Mexico, so he assumed the same would hold true for the scalphunters who worked for the Sonoran government. He had been mistaken.

The butchers had nearly wiped out the band, slaying all the women and children. Delgadito lost his family, his friends, all those who had followed him. He lost his influence among the Chiricahuas. He had been crushed, inside and out.

White Apache felt sorry for Delgadito, but he would not let his sympathy cloud his judgment. The warrior was up to something. Until White Apache learned what it was, he would treat Delgadito like a sidewinder about to strike.

"We should help the others," White Apache said. He hurried to the wagon in which the two women had been hiding. They were still there. The oldest, no more than eighteen or nineteen judging by her smooth complexion, again brandished the butcher knife and hissed at him.

"Leave us alone, devil, or I will gut you!"

White Apache glanced from one to the other. They had to be sisters. The youngest cringed behind her sibling, tears streaking her cheeks. "Come out, now," he directed.

They both acted surprised that he knew Spanish. The one with the knife draped her free arm around her sister. "Never!" she replied. "We would rather die."

White Apache pretended to ponder a moment, then shrugged. "I can see you would be too much trouble. We will leave you in peace."

Elated, the sisters looked at one another, just as White Apache counted on them doing. Instantly he leaped into the wagon. The older sister swung the knife, aiming at his groin. He blocked the blade with the Winchester, pivoted, and clubbed her with the Colt. She crumpled like soggy paper. At this the younger one gave out with a piercing scream that nearly shattered his eardrums. In disgust he grabbed her by the wrist, hauled her to the seat, and literally threw her from the wagon. She managed to land on her feet and curled into a ball, bawling like a baby.

Turning, White Apache slid the unconscious woman over his shoulder and carried her. He set her down with her back to the wheel, then stepped back.

At three other wagons, the Chiricahuas were doing the same. Everyone who had not died or fled either had to climb down or be hurled to the ground. Most chose to do it under their own power.

White Apache strode to the middle of the wagon train. "Everyone gather here, in front of me!" he commanded, stressing the point by firing a shot into the air. In seconds he got his wish as the Mexicans swiftly converged, those who could walk assisting those too petrified to move. There were only four men and they were all on in years. He counted eight women and six children. Presently three more women and one baby were added.

"That is the last of them," Cuchillo Negro announced. He studied the women, debating whether to take part or not.

At that juncture, Fiero returned, jogging out of the brush with a grin on his face and the bloody ear of a soldier in his left hand. "Look at this!" he declared, grinning. "You should have heard him screech. You would think I had cut off his manhood."

"What of the rest?" Ponce asked. All too vividly he remembered the ordeal they had been through some time ago when they were taken prisoner by the Mexicans. He did not care to see that ordeal repeated.

Fiero snorted. "They run like the scared jackrabbits they are. They will not stop until they are halfway to Guerrero." He rubbed a finger over the ear, relishing the smooth texture of the skin. It was too bad he did not have a son to give it to for the boy to play with, he reflected. In a day or so the flesh would start to rot and he would have to throw his prize away.

White Apache held the .44-40 in the crook of an elbow and paced back and forth in front of the knot of apprehensive captives. "The fight is over. Give us no more trouble," he stated, "and we will let you live."

"Liar!"

The woman he had slugged had revived. Blood trickled from her split, puffy lower lip as she shook a fist at him.

"Do not play games with us, bastard. We know how Apaches love to torture their victims! Butcher us now and be done with it!"

Some of the other travelers shushed her, telling her to be quiet before she got them all killed, but the raven-haired beauty paid no heed.

Walking closer to her, White Apache leaned down. "So you think I am an Apache, do you, girl?"

Uncertainty etched the spitfire's face. "What are you getting at? Of course you are an Apache. I am not blind."

"Look at my eyes."

"What?" the woman said, her own narrowing. "I do not see what—" She broke off, horror replacing her arrogance. "Mother of God!" she exclaimed. "The White Apache!"

Recognition sent a lightning bolt of unbridled fear tearing through the group. They huddled closer together, many crossing themselves. A heavy set woman fainted. A small boy, who until that moment had held his head high in defiance, took to crying silently.

Another woman, one with more wrinkles than a withered prune, boldly hobbled on a cane to the forefront. "I have lived longer than any of these others, so perhaps that is why I am not as afraid as they are. What is it you want with us? We have little money and hardly anything worth stealing. Speaking for myself, I am crippled and cannot walk very far. As useless as I am, it would be best to leave me here."

Fiero choked off her words by taking a step forward and putting a hand on his knife. He'd had enough of her prattle and intended to slit her throat, but he stopped short at a gesture from Lickoyee-shis-inday.

Clay Taggart was more amused than riled. The feisty crone reminded him of his grandmother, whose mouth, family members maintained, never shut for more than ten seconds at a stretch. "Do not harm her," he said in the Chiricahua tongue. "A warrior must respect courage wherever he finds it."

Smiling, Clay said in Spanish, "Please, old one. Being brave is one thing, knowing when to keep one's mouth shut another. The next time you are caught by Apaches, less talk will let you live longer."

The woman sniffed. "My name is Margarita, not 'old one'. I have lived long enough, thank you. My skin is falling from my body, all my joints ache when I move, and my eyesight is not what it used to be. My mouth is the only thing which still works as it should, and I intend to go on using it until I have nothing left to say."

White Apache laughed and pointed at the wagon. "You will live to flap your gums many more days, Margarita. Step aside so we may get this over with."

A tall man in expensive clothes, inspired by the old woman's example, moved forward. "Mister, I can tell that you are not as evil as everyone says you are. Instead of being like the rest of these savages, you show evidence of having a kind heart and a civil nature. I am Ramon Sanchez. Perhaps you have heard of me? I can make it very worth your while if you will insure that I am spared along with this old hag."

White Apache shot him. At point-blank range he pointed the Winchester, paused a fraction of a second just to see the budding terror in the man's eyes, and fired. Sanchez flew back into the wagon, leaving a scarlet smear in his wake as he slid to the earth.

The rest of the Mexicans were riveted in place, eyes as wide as walnuts, hands clasped to throats.

Except for Margarita. "If I may be so brazen, why did you do such a thing?"

No answer was forthcoming. Clay Taggart was not about to confess that he had killed the smug weasel because rich Ramon Sanchez had reminded him of rich Miles Gillett, the man who had stolen his ranch and his woman. Instead, he turned to Ponce and said, "Pick one."

The young warrior had been waiting impatiently for the selection to begin. White Apache had promised they would take turns, to make it fair for everyone, and he had secretly worried that one of the others would pick the one he wanted before he got the chance. Moving over to the young woman whose lips had swollen to the size of red peppers, he said in thickly accented Spanish, "You come with me, ish-tia-nay. You are mine now. You listen to me."

The woman recoiled as if the warrior's hand were a snake. "Don't touch me!" she cried. "I would rather die! Do not lay a finger on me, demon!"

Ponce didn't argue the point. She was his captive to do with as he saw fit, and he saw fit to smack her right across the mouth so hard that she fell onto her bottom with blood gushing from her pulped lips. Again he held out his hand. "Come now. No more talk."

Livid, the young woman made as if to punch him but thought better of it. Sullenly, she stood. She took a step, then stopped, jabbed a thumb at her sibling, and croaked, "This is my sister, Juanita Mendez. I am Maria." Grimacing, she lightly touched her mouth. "What will happen to her?"

"I cannot say," Ponce responded, and he was sincere. White Apache led the band and White Apache had not told him what was to be done with those who were not picked.

"Is she to be killed?" Maria asked. "If that is the case, take both of us. I will not go if you do not, no matter what you do to me."

Ponce was in a quandary. There had been no talk of taking more than one female apiece. He was tempted to hit her again, to show the other warriors that he would not stand for being questioned by a mere captive when their leader addressed him.

"Take both if you want. But the women must understand that if one of them cannot keep up, that one will be left to die."

Maria Mendez tenderly placed a palm on Juanita's head. "Did you hear him, sister? Perhaps it is best if you stay here, after all."

"No!" Juanita wailed, and threw herself at her sister's legs. "Don't leave me! Please! I couldn't bear it without you! Mother and father are both dead. I would be all alone!"

Maria nervously glanced at the young warrior. "All right. All right. Get on your feet, then."

As the sisters shuffled to the northwest on the heels of Ponce, Cuchillo Negro, without being told it was his turn, marched into the group, clamped a hand on the wrist of a woman in her thirties, and led her away.

White Apache was mildly surprised. Cuchillo Negro was always the quietest of the band, the man who never let his true feelings show. The warrior had voiced few comments when White Apache first proposed the idea, and until that moment he had not known if Cuchillo Negro would take part.

Delgadito went next. A woman with a big bosom had caught his eye. His wife had been flat-chested, and he had often wondered what it would be like to have a woman amply endowed.

Last to pick was Fiero. He had no interest in having a woman, but since all the others had one, he figured that he should share in the plunder. A skinny thing in a plaid dress with streaks of gray in her hair was the one he picked. His reasoning was that so thin a woman must not have much stamina, so he would not have to put up with her for very long.

White Apache waited until the Chircahuas and their captives were well on their way. Backing up, he made sure none of the Mexicans drew a hideout before he spun and jogged into the haze.

For the longest while not one of the wagon train members spoke. Margarita broke their stunned state by saying, "That was it? All they wanted was women?" She sighed as only a woman of her years could. "When we reach Janos, we must go to the church and pray for their souls. I doubt anyone will ever see them alive again."

Chapter Three

Wes Cody knew someone was coming to pay him a visit long before he saw or heard the rider. His first hint was the strident cry of a red hawk soaring above the canyon mouth. Next a flock of birds took wing from a stand of trees bordering the trail. And finally Lobo let out with a wavering howl and started to rise.

"Stay," Cody said sharply, pausing to study the piece of wood he had been whittling on for the better part of an hour.

The old wolf growled but obeyed, lowering onto its haunches. Its long tongue lolled from its mouth as it tilted its head to sniff.

"You should know who it is by now," Cody chided. "How many times does my grandson have to pay us a visit before you get it through your hairy noggin that he's not a darned hostile?"

Lobo whined and laid flat. He had spent many an hour listening to the man drone on and on, making sounds which had no meaning but which soothed him when he was troubled. Long ago he had learned that this two-leg, alone among its kind, would never harm him. This two-leg was the only one he could trust.

Presently the horseman came around a bend and let out with a hearty hail. "Grandpa! Guess who's here?"

Cody looked and frowned. There were times when the boy worried him some. It made no sense for Timothy to ask such a perfectly silly question since it was as plain as the nose on his face who was there. "Howdy, boy," he said in greeting.

Tim rode up and ground-hitched his sorrel. He was hot and tired from the long ride, and a bit irritable. "I wish you wouldn't call me that anymore, Gramps. I'm eighteen now. I'm not no boy."

"Is that a fact?" Cody said, squinting up at the tall drink of water and trying to recollect how long ago it had been when his own upper lip had been adorned with peach fuzz. "Well, I grant you that you're built mighty high above your toes, but it takes more than size to make a man." He paused. "Have you figured out what you aim to do with your life yet?"

"Not yet, but—"

"Have you found a filly to wed so you can carry on the family line?"

"No, but there—"

"Have you killed your first man yet? Fought an Injun? Taken on a bear with nothing but a knife?" Cody rattled off a string of accomplishments. "Hell, have you ever been so alkalied from red-eye that you couldn't take a step without gettin' seasick?"

Frowning, Tim took off his Stetson and mopped his brow with his red bandanna. "We've been all through this a dozen times before, Gramps. I don't see what any of that has to do with being a man. Pa's never killed anyone, not even an Indian. And he says it's how much money you make and how much influence you have that really counts."

Placing the wood in his lap, Cody scratched his white whiskers. "My main failure is that boy of mine. For the life of me, I can't rightly figure out how the blazes he turned out the way he did. I thought he'd take after me and become a scout for the Army. But no, Frank went to work in a bank, for God's sake. And then he ran for a seat on the town council." He swatted at a fly which had alighted on his buckskins. "That can't be my blood pumpin' in his veins. If I didn't know better, I'd swear his ma was foolin' around on me when I was off on patrol."

Tim Cody had heard this all before, so he merely grinned wryly and replied, "You know as well as I do that Grandma never cheated on you once during the thirty-seven years the two of you were together. She was a fine lady." The young man could not resist an appropriate barb. "What I can't savvy is what she saw in you, Gramps. The two of you were as different as night and day."

"Sometimes that's what it takes to make a marriage work," Cody declared, unruffled. "Two people who see eye-to-eye on everything would bore one another to death. There would be no surprises, no tiffs, no romance."

The young man did a double-take. "Did I hear you right? There's a smidgen of romance hiding under that crusty old hide of yours? Maybe you're the one who should be rustling up a wife."

Cody laughed and smacked his thigh. "Damn, boy. You come up with some dandies." He bobbed a chin at the open door. "Help yourself to the jug and we'll chaw a spell. It's been a coon's age since I had me a visitor."

"That's because you're too damn cantankerous for your own good," Tim said as he entered. "If you were nicer to folks, maybe more would come see you."

"Who needs them?" Cody retorted. "If I'd wanted hordes of people pokin' their noses into my affairs, I'd be livin' in Tucson instead of out here where a man can stretch his arms without feelin' crowded."

Uncorked jug in hand, Tim walked back out and plopped into a spare rickety chair. "Stretch your arms?" he said, incredulous, gazing out over the vast expanse of wilderness which surrounded the cabin. "Hell, Gramps. Your nearest neighbor is fifteen miles away. You could stretch from now until doomsday and never rub elbows with another living soul."

Cody nodded. "And that's just how I like it. A man has to have his privacy, boy. You remember that. Cities and towns are no good. They make a body feel all cooped up inside. The next thing you know, folks are at each other's throats like a pack of mad dogs."

"If you say so," Tim said. His first swallow of the homemade whiskey had the same effect it always did; he coughed, sputtered, doubled over, and thought his chest was on fire. "Are you making this stronger than usual?" he asked when his vocal chords worked again.

"That jug has been sittin' longer than most," Cody said. Taking it, he drank in deep gulps, sighed loudly in contentment, and smacked his lips. "Not bad, if I do say so myself. It sure is tastier than that watered down coffin varnish they pass for whiskey in the saloons. Why, that stuff isn't good for anything except garglin' with." He passed the jug back. "So you haven't told me. What brings you out to see me? You just feelin' sociable?"

The young man's eyebrows arched. "I don't reckon I like the way you put that, seeing as how I'm the only one who ever goes to all the trouble to come here. Pa can't be bothered. He says it will teach you a lesson."

"How's that?"

"He figures that sooner or later you'll get tired of living like a hermit and move into town where civilized folks ought to be."

Cody sadly shook his head. "Definitely no blood kin of mine. Or maybe it was that fall he took when he was four and I was tryin' to teach him how to ride. He did hit his head awful hard."

Tim set down the jug, unbuttoned his shirt, and pulled out a large folded sheet which he opened. "I've got something to show you, Gramps. I took it off the board in front of the marshal's office."

It was a Wanted Poster. The scout read it, moving his lips as he did, his brow puckered. "I've heard of this feller. Imagine the whole Territory has by now." He shook the sheet. "But what does this have to do with anything?"

"Did you see how much they're offering?"

"Ten thousand dollars, dead or alive," Cody quoted. "Lord, that is a lot of money. I can't recall any badman ever being worth that much before. Bounty hunters must be swarming to Arizona from all over the country."

"So I've heard," Tim said. He stretched his long legs and mulled over how best to bring up the subject which had prompted his visit. "Billy Santee went after him but came back with his tail tucked between his legs."

Cody snickered. "Santee, the gunfighter? Hell, boy, that jasper couldn't track a bull buffalo through a mud wallow. The only thing he can do well is shoot, and against the sort of hombre he was after, that don't amount to a hill of beans."

Lobo stood, yawned, and came over. He licked Tim's hand, receiving a few tentative pats in return. The wolf smelled a faint trace of fear, but that was normal for the young two-leg.

Had the animal but known, Tim Cody was scared to death of it. Since childhood he'd heard harrowing tales of incidents where wolves tore unwary travelers to bits. His grandfather branded such stories as pure hogwash, but Tim couldn't shake a feeling of unease every time the wolf was near him. Clearing his throat, he said, "Maybe you have a point about Santee. But how about Quick Killer, the scout? He went after the bastard, too."

Cody's interest perked considerably. "Tats-ah-das-ay-go? What happened?"

"His head turned up at Fort Bowie all by itself." Tim chuckled. "I hear tell the colonel was fit to be tied. He sent his best officer and a whole passel of soldiers out, but they showed up empty handed."

"Quick Killer," Cody said softly, impressed. He had known the half-breed fairly well, having worked with him a few times before retiring. In all his days, Cody had never met a harder man. Quick Killer had been pure snake mean but he had also been one of the best trackers in the army's employ. If anyone should have been able to do the job, Cody mused, it was Tats-ah-das-ay-go.

"That's not all," Tim went on. "Another scout by the name of Nah-kah-yen tried. He went off into the Dragoons and no one has heard from him since."

Another name that rang a bell. Cody had ridden a few patrols with Nah-kah-yen back in the days before the Chircahuas were confined to a reservation. While not as skilled as Quick Killer, Nah-kah-yen had been as dependable as the day was long.

"The talk is that the army has about given up hope. Folks expect the killing to go on for a long time."

"That's a cryin' shame," Cody acknowledged. A thought occurred to him but he discarded the fool notion. He was much too old to think about going after the butchers.

Tim leaned forward and propped his elbows on his knees. "I reckon you haven't heard the latest, Gramps. The band struck a wagon train south of the border. You'll never guess what they made off with this time."

"Horses and guns," Cody said. After all, what else would Apaches steal?

"Nope." Tim noticed the wolf eyeing the sorrel and wondered if the beast had eaten recently. "Women. It was in the *EPITAPH*. They made worm food of a lot of soldiers, killed a heap of pilgrims, and skedaddled with five women. Word was sent to the Fifth Cavalry to keep their eyes peeled but so far they haven't seen hide nor hair of those bastards."

The scout pondered a bit. "This time of year, the band is likely making for Lost Canyon. At least, that's what the scouts used to call the place."

"Never heard of it," Tim mentioned casually to hide the pounding of his heart.

"You'd have to go deep into the Dragoon Mountains to get there," Cody revealed. "The only way in is through a narrow little gap in a high cliff. There's a fifty-acre valley watered by a sizeable stream. The Apaches have been using the place for years to hide stolen stock and such. Few whites even know it's there."

The grandson made a teepee of his hands and gazed skyward. He was not a religious man but he would pray on occasion. "Could you find this Lost Canyon if you wanted to?"

"Of course I could. I know this whole part of the country better than any man alive, except maybe Al Sieber, and I taught him most of what he knows."

A peculiar gleam lit Tim's green eyes. Everything was coming together as he had hoped it would. "Say, Gramps," he said to change the subject, "any chance of my getting something to eat? I haven't had a bite since breakfast and I'm half starved." In truth, he needed time to contemplate how best to go about getting to the heart of the matter. It would be unwise to come right out and ask the question. His cranky grandfather might refuse on general principles, and once Wes Cody made a decision there was no changing his mind.

"Let's go on in and I'll whip you up some vittles," Cody proposed. "I could go for a plate or two myself. I don't eat as regular as I should, being alone and all. Most of the time I just skin me a rattler and make a right fine stew."

The thought of eating a snake made Tim squeamish. He'd done so before and never liked it. Each time he'd dipped his spoon in the bowl, he kept expecting the rattler's head to lunge out and bite him. "Is that what we'll be having?"

"No. I'm afraid you'll have to settle for some venison. I dropped a buck a couple of days ago and I don't think the meat is all rotten yet." Cody rose. "Don't forget to bring your chair in."

Tim smiled gamely and followed the older man. He said nothing, but he never had understood how his grandfather could live in such a hovel. Dust constantly blew in through cracks in the walls and the roof forever leaked when it rained. A small bench lined the east wall, a table with one leg shorter than the rest sat in the middle of the single room, and a dilapidated cot completed the collection of so-called furniture.

Brushing dust from the edge of the table so it wouldn't smear his shirt, Tim plunked down the chair and straddled it. "If pa ever saw how messy you keep your cabin, he'd cuss you a blue streak for being so lazy."

Cody had found the pan he wanted and placed it on the stove. "That's your grandma's fault. She spoiled that boy when he was young. Twice a week she'd do laundry just so he could wear a clean pair of underwear and socks every day. Every single day!" He paused, recalling how lovely his wife had looked with her sandy hair up in a bun and beads of sweat on her forehead. Now there had been a woman! "If you ask me, she spoiled your pa. I told her that it wasn't natural for a boy to have to change his underwear more than once a month, but she wouldn't listen. That's what an Eastern upbringing does to a person. Makes them so damned fussy, they take to thinkin' they should smell like lilacs all the time."

From a shelf Cody took a bag of flour and partially filled a bowl, then added water from his water skin.

"The fact is, boy, if the Good Lord had meant for us to smell like flowers, we'd have petals for hair. And if we were supposed to walk around as clean as a new rifle, the Good Lord would never have made dirt."

"You have a strange way of looking at life, Gramps," Tim commented. But it had always been thus. His earliest recollection of his grandfather was the evening Wes rode into town with three dead Apaches draped over pack horses. It had been his pa's birthday. That very morning a band of Mescaleros had been caught raiding a ranch by a patrol and been wiped out. On the spur of the moment Wes had decided to give a brand new scalp as a present. His pa got to pick the head of hair he liked the most on the three dead warriors.

Looking at his grandpa now, Tim found it hard to believe that once Wes Cody had been a name to be reckoned with. The old man had been the best scout alive, better than Kit Carson ever was according to old-timers who knew. Wes had killed scores of renegades and a few outlaws, to boot.

"No one ever said we all have to look at life the exact same way, boy. Find the way that's best for you and live like there will be no tomorrow. That's the secret to havin' no regrets."

"Oh? Do you have any regrets, other than pa, that is?"

Cody pursed his lips. "Well, now that you bring it up, I reckon there were a few things I'd change if I could go back and live my life all over again." He stirred the flour with a big wooden spoon. "But that's wishful thinkin', which is just a fancy name for moanin' and groanin' over the way things could have been."

For a while Tim was silent. The tantalizing aroma of brewing coffee filled the cabin, mingled with the delicious odor of the biscuits and thick steaks. "It's too bad you've given up scouting," he said at last. "I bet you'd bring the traitor to bay in no time."

"I wouldn't go that far," Cody said. "He's a smart one. Quick Killer was no daisy. It might take a spell, but yes, I'd nail his hide to the wall."

Tim took a deep breath. "Maybe you should, then."

"What?" Cody asked absently while checking the steaks.

"Go after the band," Tim said, and averted his gaze

when his grandfather gave him the sort of look one might give a crazed Comanche. "Think of it, Gramps. Dozens of innocent people have lost their lives already, and there's no telling how many more will go to meet their Maker before this hombre is caught or killed."

Cody was surprised by the suggestion. He hadn't tracked a man in so long, he was as rusty as could be. But he was also intrigued by the idea of getting off his backside and doing something worthwhile for a change. "I couldn't," he said lamely. "For one thing, I'm too damn old. My joints ache all the time, and I'm not as spry as I used to be."

Tim was prepared for any and every argument. "A little exercise is all you need. Once you're out and around, it will all come back to you."

"Maybe." Cody turned a biscuit over to keep it from burning. "Even so, I couldn't do it alone, not even when I was in my prime. I'd need help. And there isn't a man alive fool enough to throw in with me for a proposition like that."

"I'd go."

Cody smiled. "I appreciate the offer, son. I really do. But totin' a six-shooter and wearin' those high-heeled boots and that John B. doesn't make you an Injun fighter. It takes a special knack."

"I could learn," Tim pressed.

"Given time," Cody agreed, "which the renegades aren't about to give you. No, I'd need a couple of men who would do to ride the river with."

Trying not to become too excited, Tim played his ace in the hole. "How about Iron Eyes? He'd leap at the chance to help. And he could certainly use a share of the money."

Grabbing a pair of cracked plates, Cody forked the

two steaks onto them, added several biscuits, and brought the feast to the table. "Funny you should mention that no-account Navajo. He's the one man I could always rely on, through thick and thin. I wouldn't know where to find him, though."

"I do. He's living in a shack not far from Fort Bowie. All you'd have to do is ask."

Suddenly it dawned on Wes Cody that his grandson was taking an inordinate interest in the renegades. He studied the young man a moment. "It seems to me that you have this whole thing already worked out. This is why you came to see me, isn't it?"

"Partly," Tim admitted, knowing full well his grandfather couldn't abide a liar. Quickly he continued to plead his case. "And Iron Eyes isn't the only one interested. I've talked to Ren Starky, too. He's interested."

"Ren?" Cody said, memories flooding through him of a snot-nosed kid he had taught the ins and outs of being a scout, a man more like a son than a friend. Certainly more like a son than his own son.

"Yes, sir. He's over to Tucson. He said that if you came by and asked him personally, he'd pull up stakes and come along."

Cody leaned back, not caring that his steak was growing cold. "Been making the rounds, haven't you, boy? Settin' things up so it would be hard for me to say no."

Tim grinned slyly. "I've done my best. Always have an edge. Isn't that what you taught me?"

The boy had spunk, Cody told himself. And he had to admit that the prospect of working with Iron Eyes and Ren Starky again was awful appealing. "What about the reward, Timothy? I suppose you've given thought to that as well?"

"Split four ways. That's two thousand, five hundred dollars for each of us. More money than you've ever seen at one time in your life, Gramps. Enough to tide you over in your twilight years." Tim gestured. "You could fix this place up. Or have a new cabin built, one with a decent roof. Or maybe you'd like to have a pump put in so you don't need to lug water from the spring every time you want a drink. Then there's—"

Cody held up a weathered hand. "That's enough, boy. I swear, when you're on a tear you can prattle worse than your grandma. The Good Lord rest her soul." He yanked his Bowie knife from its sheath on his left hip, picked up the fork, and dug into the steak.

Slicing, lifting, chewing, Cody did it all automatically. He couldn't shake the notion the boy had planted, and the more he contemplated, the more he liked it. He tried telling himself that he was being a jackass, thinking he could bring in the renegades at his age. But he was old, not dead. He had a lifetime of experience to fall back on. He'd stand as good a chance as anyone else and better than most.

The money was unimportant. Cody never had any use for it, except to buy the bare necessities.

Saving a lot of lives was what interested Cody the most. All his life he had been looking out for those too weak or ignorant to look out for themselves. He'd guided wagon trains for a while, worked as a deputy sheriff, and then signed on to scout for the army, to help put the red savages in their place and make Arizona safe for white folks.

Cody cut off another chunk and bit down with relish. He had enough money cached away for the supplies they would need. And with the likes of Iron Eyes and Ren to back him up, he'd end the bloodshed once and for all. "All right, boy. You've convinced me. I must not have the sense God gave a turnip because I'm going to do it." He smiled, feeling grand to be alive. "I'm going to go after the White Apache."

Chapter Four

Their destination was a paradise nestled in the bowels of the foreboding Dragoon Mountains, an oasis of grass and water in the midst of a parched inferno, one of several such sanctuaries known only to Apaches.

This one was considered the safest. No white man had ever been there, so far as Clay Taggart's Chiricahua companions knew. They need not be on their guard all the time. They could relax, rest up. Best of all, the new members of the band would have time to adjust to their new lot in life.

It was not an easy adjustment, Clay Taggart knew. The five Mexican women had been torn from all that was familiar and violently thrust into the terror of the unknown. In a span of minutes their lives had turned topsy-turvy, and it would never be the same again.

Predictably, the five went into various degrees of shock that first day after leaving the wagon train. They had to be goaded on, often with threats, sometimes with blows. Each warrior was responsible for the woman he had chosen, and since Clay had not picked one, he had little to do but keep his eyes skinned for enemies. He could observe all that went on and assess the captives for himself.

The two sisters were as different as two people could be and still be kin. Maria reminded him of a mustang which had never been broken. She was brazen, defiant, and proud. Without complaint, she did her best to keep up, her back stiff, her chin thrust out as if it were a lance.

Juanita, on the other hand, cringed if Ponce so much as looked at her crosswise and whined like a whipped puppy if he so much as touched her. That first day out, she gave them more trouble than all the others combined. She was weak in body as well as mind. Tiring readily, again and again she fell behind, her head hung low, sniffling in misery.

Again and again Ponce had to hurry her along. Initially he used sharp words and that sufficed. But as the day dragged on, Juanita's shock deepened to where she plodded along as one already dead. For perhaps the tenth time she dropped a dozen yards to the rear.

Ponce stomped back, annoyed at himself for having agreed to bring her along, grabbed her by the arm, and pushed. "Go fast," he commanded. "Soldiers maybe come."

Juanita turned dull eyes on him. She made no attempt to obey but stood there as if deaf and dumb.

"Faster, Ish-tia-nay!" Ponce growled. He was keenly conscious of the stares of the older warriors and anxious to show that he could keep his women in line. Among Apaches it was unthinkable for a woman to shame her man. No warrior would stand for it. So when this woman did nothing more than stare blankly at him, he slapped her. The blow knocked Juanita to her knees. She made no sound other than a pathetic whimper. Nor did she stand and trek onward as he wanted.

"You are good for nothing," Ponce spat in disgust.

Clay Taggart had to agree. From an Apache standpoint, she was truly good for nothing. He saw the young warrior raise a fist to strike her down.

"No!" Maria Mendez shouted, darting over and flinging herself between the Chiricahua and her sister. "Please! I will see to it that she does not give you a problem from now on." She put her hands on Ponce's upraised arm. "Please!" she repeated softly, looking him right in the eyes.

"Beat them both," Fiero suggested. "Women must be taught to do as they are told."

Ponce hesitated. He was angry enough to beat the pair. He wanted to strike them. But when he gazed into the piercing, pleading eyes of the pretty one, his insides twisted all up and he felt as if he could hardly breathe. It was a strange feeling, one he had never known before, and he did not know what to make of it. In his confusion he lowered his arm, collected his wits, and grunted. "Very well, woman," he growled in his imperfect Spanish. "Make sister come. Make her walk fast." He stalked onward.

That had been Clay's first clue that Ponce might have bitten off more than he could chew. Juanita was docile enough, but Maria was a wolf in sheep's clothing, a woman who could hold her own against any man, and who probably would use every manner of persuasion at her command to get what she wanted. He predicted to himself that within a moon Ponce would be fawning over her, bringing her all manner of trinkets and blankets and whatever else in plunder she desired.

The other women did much better than Juanita. By the second day they had recovered enough to whisper among themselves during short halts called so they could rest.

Delgadito's choice, the woman with the big chest, was named Alexandra. She had sleek hair and a sway to her hips which was a marvel for him to behold. She pleased him greatly by doing whatever he told her without protest, but she had a habit of cringing when he sat close and once bit her lip when he touched her neck.

Florencio was the name of the woman chosen by Cuchillo Negro. He had picked well. She adapted much more quickly than the rest. By the fourth day she was trying to learn the Chiricahua tongue and would point objects out for him to name. On the sixth night they went off together and did not come back until first light.

The other women would have nothing to do with Florencio for two days afterward.

But the biggest surprise of all was the woman Fiero had taken. Delores Garcia hardly ever said a word. When the firebrand told her to do something, she did it right away. She had superb endurance and was the least tired at the end of a long day. When the other women were gasping with fatigue, she was not even breathing hard.

Fiero admitted it to no one, but he was amazed at how well she did. She was so thin, so frail, yet she endured. Initially, it angered him. He had not wanted a woman and had no intention of keeping her. Day after day he looked for her to keel over so he could go on alone, but she seemed to grow stronger, not weaker. It was a great mystery to him. He held the Nakai-yes in contempt as weaklings and cowards, yet here this skinny woman was proving to be made of tempered steel.

White Apache pushed hard for the border. The Mexican Army was bound to try and cut them off, and once on U.S. soil they would be safe. His only worry was that word would reach Arizona before they got there and the Fifth Cavalry would try to intercept them before they could reach the Dragoons.

Sure enough, the band crossed over east of Nogales and almost immediately came on fresh tracks of many shod horses moving in a column from east to west.

White Apache changed tactics. Instead of traveling north from dawn until dust, they holed up in gullies or thick brush during the day and moved only at night. They were hours shy of the Dragoon Mountains when that which he wanted to avoid, happened.

It was almost dawn. White Apache sought a place to lay low. He was in the lead, scanning the chaparral, when he came to a low hill and trudged to the top. Only when he paused on the crest did he realize the blunder he had almost made.

Encamped at the base of the hill was a patrol. To the east the mounts had been tethered. The troopers still slept except for a pair of sentries and a man busy making coffee. In another few minutes reveille would be sounded.

The hill had not only hidden the camp, it had muffled what little noise was being made. And the thin tendrils of smoke from the fire were being blown around the hill, not over it.

White Apache immediately crouched and motioned. The warriors imitated him, pulling the women down beside them. He saw that neither sentry had

seen him, while the man at the fire was wrestling with
a can which would not open. Backing quietly down
the slope, he was almost below the rim when one of
the sentries happened to glance up.

The soldier was a private, a very young and inexperienced private who had arrived at Fort Bowie less
than two weeks before. This was his first patrol and
he was as tightly wound as a spring. On spying the
head of a figure silhouetted against the brightening
sky, he did what came naturally; he whipped his carbine to his shoulder and banged off a shot.

White Apache ducked a heartbeat before bits of dirt
rained down on him. Sprinting to the left, he joined
the band as the warriors hauled the captives into the
brush.

The women had been hiking all night and were ex-
tremely tired. They were also bewildered by the gun-
shot and the reaction of their captors. Juanita Mendez
was so scared she could scarcely move, so Maria took
it on herself to hurry her along.

Pandemonium reigned in the camp. White Apache
heard bellows and the rattle of accoutrements. He
jogged farther into the mesquite, careful to avoid the
thorny limbs. The brush slowed them down, but it
also worked in their favor. No self-respecting cavalryman would plunge his horse into mesquite and have
it ripped to ribbons.

They covered about 100 yards when pursuit
sounded. Horses nickered, hooves drummed, and an
officer rasped orders. "Jenkins, take your men to the
right. Wilson, to the left. Spread out. We'll trap them
between us." Almost as an afterthought, the man
added, "Chivari, you know what to do."

White Apache stopped. It was nice of the officer to
let them know what the troopers were up to. Their

only hope lay in covering a lot of ground before the net tightened. He ran, but not at his top speed because the women couldn't sustain the same pace.

To the north and the south, cavalrymen were doing as they had been told. White Apache glimpsed several.

So did Fiero, who fingered his rifle, longing to open fire. He had vowed to slay as many whites as he could before Yusn saw fit to take him, and he was loathe to pass up any chance to drop a few. In frustration, he kicked Delores when she went too slow to suit him.

Ponce had his hands full. Juanita kept lagging, as always, and he had to pull on her arm over and over. Once he went to backhand her but Maria, ever alert, leaped between them. And no matter how mad he might be, he couldn't bring himself to hit the older one. It upset him, this weakness of his.

The mesquite thinned. White Apache could tell the troopers were 40 to 50 feet behind on both sides and had yet to close the net. The band was almost in the clear. A wide gap opened to the northwest and he took it.

Somewhere in the brush behind them, a twig snapped.

White Apache halted to look back. He wondered if some of the troopers were on foot. It was no cause for alarm as most soldiers had all the woodcraft of a rock. They couldn't track, they couldn't shoot very well, and they couldn't move silently if their lives depended on it. Eluding them would not be difficult.

The other members of the band also heard the sound. Fiero, last in line, whispered to Ponce, "Watch my woman." Then he melted into the chaparral.

Only Ponce saw him go. The young warrior had no desire to burden himself with a third female when it was all he could do to keep Maria and Juanita from falling behind, but he was not about to say no and risk angering Fiero. It was common knowledge that those who displeased Fiero sometimes wound up being challenged to formal combat on one pretext or another. It was also common knowledge that Fiero always won.

White Apache had no idea that the firebrand was no longer with them. On coming to an open tract, he pointed at a line of brush 40 yards away and whispered in Spanish, "Get under cover, pronto."

The clump of hooves grew steadily nearer. White Apache spotted a cavalryman 60 or 70 feet distant, to the northeast. Crouching, he covered the rest with his Winchester as they hastened on by. When Ponce came abreast of him with three women instead of two, he made a head count and checked an urge to curse a blue streak.

"Where is Fiero?" White Apache demanded.

"He went to kill white-eyes," Ponce answered.

"Damn that yack," White Apache grumbled to himself in English. "I swear he doesn't have the brains of a cactus." To Ponce he said, "Tell Delgadito to go head north. I will catch up as soon as I can."

Slipping into the chaparral, White Apache went a few yards, then ducked down and watched the band cover the open tract. Once they were safe, he turned to go after Fiero. As he did, a rider materialized to his right, not more than 20 feet away. It was the first of a long line of troopers. Another was approaching on the left. Soon they would meet up and the trap would be complete.

Slipping into the brush, White Apache stayed low. Thanks to his Chiricahua mentor, he could move almost as silently as a full-blooded warrior. Being sure not to rustle the vegetation or snag the rifle, he worked his way steadily deeper into the patch of mesquite.

To the west a man hollered. "We've met up, Captain. We have them ringed in."

"Stay on your guard," the commanding officer shouted. "They're liable to make a break for it at any moment. Leave them to Chivari."

That made twice the officer had mentioned the same name. An Indian name. White Apache suspected it might be the name of an Indian scout since the army had long been hiring bored reservation warriors and warriors from other tribes to help hunt renegades down, a program which had proved very successful. Hunkering, he surveyed the mesquite, but not so much as a shadow moved.

Meanwhile, the soldiers were slowly closing in from all sides. Their carbines gleamed in the pale glow of the rising sun. Many were in a state of undress, with shirts half buttoned or not tucked in, pants hanging out over the tops of boots, and disheveled hair. Most were young, no more than 19 or 20, and plenty scared although trying hard not to show it.

Suddenly White Apache detected a hint of motion ahead of him. Going to ground, he examined the spot, noting the outline of plants, seeking a shape which didn't fit.

So far the sun had merely peeked above the horizon. The mesquite still lay in shadow. But soon, very soon, the golden orb would light up the sky. White Apache had to get out of there before that happened.

Moments passed. White Apache spied someone slinking through the vegetation. He was about to whisper, thinking it was Ponce, when the person turned toward him and he saw that it was a warrior in an army uniform, a scout, but from which tribe he could not say. He caught only a hint of the man's surprised expression and they both brought up their rifles at the same time.

A stocky form rose up as if from out of nowhere and bore the scout to the earth. There was a flurry of movement, the dull flash of a blade, and a low grunt.

Fiero rose from the body, grinning in triumph, his knife dripping red drops. He started forward.

White Apache checked on the troopers. None were close enough to have heard. They were scouring the mesquite, moving slowly so as not to harm their mounts, carbines cocked and at the ready. If he and Fiero used all their skill, they should be able to slip through the line without being caught.

Then White Apache looked at the hothead and saw another figure rising behind him, in the act of bringing a rifle to bear. Without thinking, he blasted a shot from the hip and struck the second scout in the chest. The Indian flipped backwards.

Fiero whirled, elevating his knife. He saw the quivering body and went to voice his gratitude when a strident yell reminded them both that they were still in the gravest danger.

"In there! I see an Apache!"

A carbine cracked, the first discordant note in a lethal symphony as the troopers cut loose from all sides, peppering the mesquite. Few of them saw a target to shoot at but that did not stop them from firing. Their nerves had been stretched to the breaking point at the mere thought of going up against the terrors of the Southwest. Any excuse to shoot was welcome and they took it.

White Apache and Fiero, bent at the waist, sped westward, hugging the thickest clusters of mesquite. Bullets clipped branches on all sides and tore into the earth around them. It reminded White Apache of being caught in the middle of a hailstorm, only this storm was leaden, not balls of ice, and would do more than sting.

Only one thing saved them. Most of the troopers poured fire into the spot pointed out by the first cavalryman, which happened to be slightly to the right of where Fiero had been standing. In short order, White Apache and the Chiricahua were a score of yards from the center of the withering volley. Fewer and fewer slugs came anywhere near them. They were out of the frying pan, but far from out of the fire.

Ahead of them were more troopers, firing carbines like men possessed.

White Apache sank to a knee behind a bush and sought a gap in the line through which they could sneak. There was none. The cavalrymen were spaced too closely together for them to get through.

Fiero was crouched low close by. He smiled grimly at the sight of the American soldiers. There were too many for Lickoyee-shis-inday and him to defeat or evade. His time had come. So be it. He had long known that one day he would die in battle, and he was prepared. At least he would be able to fulfill his yearning to take as many of the hated white-eyes with him as he could before they slew him.

White Apache saw his companion begin to take aim and he smacked the barrel down. "No," he said. "I will lead them off. You must catch up with the others. They will need your help with the women."

"What do they matter to me?" Fiero countered testily.

"They should matter to all of us," White Apache persisted. "Without them, we cannot rebuild the band. We need those women more than they know."

To forestall an argument, White Apache veered to

the right toward a soldier who appeared to be one of the youngest. The trooper had stopped firing and was frantically reloading, his head bent to his carbine when he should have been watching the brush surrounding him.

White Apache glanced at the cavalrymen on either side of the youth, insured neither of them had seen him, and surged from cover. In a lithe bound he reached the trooper's bay and drove the barrel of the Winchester into the young man's gut. Uttering a squawk, the trooper went flying. It was but an instant's work for White Apache to grab the saddle horn, swing into the stirrups, and wheel the startled bay even as he swiveled in the saddle and shot the soldier on his right. Then, bending low over the animal's neck, he applied his heels and broke into a gallop.

"There he goes!"

"He shot Simmons!"

"Stop him!"

"Kill him!"

The chorus of shouts preceded another ragged volley. White Apache felt a searing pain in his calf and looked down to see a thin red line where he had been creased. A resounding smack told him the bay had also been hit but apparently the wound wasn't mortal for the horse raced northward as if a grizzly nipped at its tail.

From all points the troopers gave chase, winding though the mesquite, firing on the fly. The swaying and bouncing of their animals made accuracy next to impossible but they fired anyway.

White Apache cut to the left, then the right. Constantly weaving, he hoped to keep from having the bay shot out from under him. Should that happen, he had no illusions about the outcome. This time the caval-

rymen would know right where to find him and would
be on him before he could drop more than one or two.
In a roundabout way, Miles Gillett would have won,
and he would be damned if he was going to let that
happen.

The officer shouted more orders but they were
drowned out by the shots and the thunder of so many
hooves.

Rather abruptly the chaparral tapered off and was
replaced by a flat plain dotted with brown grass.
White Apache let the horse have its head. A mile away
reared a series of low hills. Reaching them was his
sole hope.

Whooping and cursing and shooting wildly, the
troopers burst from the mesquite in an uneven line
and lashed their mounts. At their center rode the officer, a captain.

"Cease firing! You're wasting ammo!" he roared.

The firing dwindled as the word was passed. Clay
knuckled down to the task of staying ahead of them.
The bay ran superbly, mane and tail flying, until they
were two-thirds of the way across when it suddenly
broke stride, faltered and nearly went down.

White Apache wrenched on the reins. The animal
recovered and galloped just as hard as before, but its
breathing was quite labored. Shifting, he saw a crim-
son rivulet flowing from under the saddle and down
over its belly. The wound was more severe than he had
thought.

Now the crucial issue was whether the horse had
enough strength left to reach the hills. They were
wooded and creased with washes and ravines. White
Apache could give the cavalrymen the slip, if only he
could get there! Slowly but surely, though, the troopers were gaining. Some of them sensed they were

close to catching him and yipped for joy.

The hills loomed closer, yet oh, so far. White Apache spoke softly to the horse, urging it on, but his words were in vain. He was still 100 yards shy of them when the bay's front legs buckled.

Chapter Five

White Apache hurled himself free of the saddle the instant the horse started to go into a forward roll. His left shoulder bore the brunt of the fall, jarring his torso with excrutiating pain. Sheer momentum carried him a dozen feet. His right knee glanced off a rock, spearing agony up and down his leg. No sooner did he come to rest than he shoved to his feet.

The bay had done a complete roll and wound up upright, wheezing like a bellows. It was winded and wounded but still alive, which was all that mattered.

To slow down the cavalrymen, White Apache squeezed off two swift shots at the middle of the charging line. One of the troopers twisted and nearly went down. Others angled to either side.

White Apache dashed to the bay and vaulted into the saddle. Some of his pursuers opened fire but their shots zinged wide of the mark. Slapping his legs as hard as he could, he goaded the bay into a lurching gallop. Within a few strides it settled into an easy lope but it still breathed noisily and was clearly on its last legs.

By now the hill was so close that White Apache was under the illusion he could reach out and touch it. The troopers had gained a lot of ground, though, and he would be hard pressed to reach cover before they were on him. To guarantee he could, he swiveled and blasted away, emptying the Winchester in a flurry of shots which broke the charging line and caused the troopers to scatter to the right and the left.

Then White Apache reached the hill and swept around it. In seconds he was screened from the troopers, but that would not last long. He must act quickly.

Plenty of brush grew on its slope but nowhere was it thick enough to suit White Apache's urgent purpose. Fate had conspired to thwart him. The troopers would either shoot him to ribbons or overwhelm him and cart him to Fort Bowie to stand trial and be publicly executed. His luck had finally run out.

Just as the thought crossed White Apache's mind, he saw a cleft in the side of the hill. It wasn't long and it wasn't wide but it would have to do. Hauling on the reins, he brought the bay to a sliding stop. He jumped down, gave the horse a smack on the rump with the Winchester, and bent at the cleft as it ran off. By turning sideways he found that he could squeeze into the gap. It was a tight fit. Projecting spines of rough stone gouged and scraped him. One tore into his cheek and drew blood.

Hardly was White Apache in place than the lead troopers thundered past. The dust of their passage choked the air, becoming steadily thicker as more and more cavalrymen did the same. Spreading rapidly, it soon covered the cleft. White Apache could no longer see the soldiers going by but he could hear them, and only after the drum of hooves faded did he wriggle his way loose and rise.

The desperate ruse had worked. But White Apache knew it would not be long before the cavalrymen over-took the riderless bay. They would fan out and back-track, poking into every nook and cranny. He had to get out of there.

He sprinted into the dust, retracing his steps. The last thing the soldiers would ever expect would be for him to try and cross the plain on foot, but that was exactly what he intended to do.

Abruptly, White Apache heard another horse com-ing from the plain. It had to be a straggler, and the man was heading straight for him. The swirling dust prevented him from seeing the trooper, but it also hid him. He hunkered down, hoping the man would not catch a glimpse of him. He should have known better.

Out of the dusty veil appeared the rider, the very trooper White Apache had clipped in the shoulder. The man was pale, his uniform shirt caked with blood. He was having trouble staying in the saddle. Yet on spotting the White Apache, he mustered enough en-ergy to raise his carbine.

White Apache dared not let the gun go off. It would bring the patrol on the run. He would have to try and lose them all over again and this time they would not be so easy to trick.

Rushing the wounded cavalryman, White Apache sprang high into the air and slammed the Winchester against the trooper's head. His swing was a little off or he would have caved in the man's skull. As it was, the soldier toppled, unconscious, and the horse slowed to a stop.

White Apache wasted no time. He forked leather, cut the reins, and raced for the plain. It was clear of troopers. Making to the southwest, he pushed the horse mercilessly. Every few seconds he checked behind him. The patrol failed to appear and much to his relief he gained the cover of the chaparral.

Halting in a wash, White Apache fed cartridges into the Winchester. In turn, he verified each pistol had five pills in the wheel.

Cutting the band's trail proved to be no problem.

Apaches left few tracks, since from early childhood they honed the craft of moving stealthily. As soon as they could walk, they were taught to always step where the ground was hardest and to apply most of their weight to the balls of their feet so they would leave no prints or impartial tracks at best. The four Chiricahuas were masters of the art.

But the captives were another story. The women left as clear a trail as would a small herd of cattle. White Apache turned to the north and maintained a trot for over half a mile.

The warriors were waiting for him. They heard a horse approaching long before it came into sight, and took cover, Ponce and Cuchillo Negro guarding the women while Delgadito and Fiero concealed themselves where the brush narrowed.

Fiero had only just caught up with the others. Storm clouds were imminent on his brow, and with good reason. He had been upset when White Apache told him to lie there in the dirt while White Apache led the soldiers off. Lickoyee-shis-inday had treated him as if he were an inexperienced warrior out on his very first raid. Worse, it had been a command, not a request, and no man had the right to give an order to an Apache, not even another Apache.

Unlike the white-eyes and the Nakai-yes, the Chiricahuas and other Apaches regarded no one as their masters. While it was true each tribe had leaders, these leaders were not like those of the Sioux or the Cheyenne or the Arapaho. They were not chiefs in the strict meaning of the word.

Apache leaders led by virtue of their superior cunning and skill. They were allowed to lead because other warriors acknowledged their ability and respected their judgment. But at no time did an Apache leader have the right to tell another warrior what to do. A leader might suggest. A leader might argue. A leader might cajole. But a leader never, ever, commanded, not in the way the officers in the American and Mexican armies commanded troops, and not in the way chiefs of other tribes sometimes ordered the warriors under them.

For as long as there had been the earth and sky, the Apaches had prided themselves on their independence. Each warrior was his own master, answerable to no one other than himself. If a given band wanted to go on the war path but one or two men did not care to join in the raid, it was their right to stay behind. An Apache always had the choice of saying 'no'.

White Apache had denied Fiero that right, and he was not one to overlook the slight. He meant to bring the issue to a head, so he was glad to see Lickoyee-shis-inday heading toward him on a stolen cavalry mount. Stepping into the open to bar the horse from going further, he declared gruffly, "We must talk."

Clay Taggart was surprised. He knew the firebrand well enough to know that Fiero was angry. Over what, he couldn't imagine. Under different circumstances hearing the warrior out would not have posed a problem, but the patrol was much too close and would soon be scouring the area. "Can your words wait for a better time?" he asked as he slid down.

From out of the undergrowth came the others. The women, sensing sudden tension in the air, hung back. The warriors, puzzled, made no move to intervene.

Of them all, Cuchillo Negro was the most concerned. Fiero's temper was not to be taken lightly. Too many times had he seen Fiero fly into a rage over the most trivial of matters, with unfortunate consequences to the one who had offended him.

Cuchillo Negro would not permit Lickoyee-shis-inday to be harmed. The future of the band, perhaps the future of the entire Chiricahua tribe, rested on White Apache's unsuspecting shoulders. Stepping to one side, he cradled his rifle and used his sleeve to muffle the click as he slowly pulled back the hammer.

Unaware of this, Fiero was saying, "No, they cannot. We must settle this now. You have gone too far. I will not be insulted again."

There were times when Clay Taggart had to control an urge to slug the arrogant warrior in the mouth. Of late, Fiero had made a habit of challenging him practically every time he made a decision, and he was growing tired of it. "Explain," he said.

"You have lived among us many sleeps. You know the ways of the Shis-Inday as well as you do those of your own kind," Fiero began.

"This is true," White Apache said when the other paused, to goad him along.

"So it is that you know the Shis-Inday are not like other men. We do not let another tell us what we should do and when we should do it. Always are we free to do as we please."

This, too, was true. White Apache waited for the hothead to get to the point while listening intently. It was doubtful the troopers were anywhere near, but it didn't pay to take anything for granted.

"Back there," Fiero said, pointing, "you stopped me from shooting an American as I wanted to do. You were wrong to do so." He paused. "You also ordered me to stay while you led the soldiers away. You were wrong to do so."

"We were surrounded. They were shooting at us. I had to act fast. There was no time to talk it over," White Apache said, irritated that the warrior would quibble over such a point.

"You should not have knocked my gun down. You should not have made me do that which I did not want to do." Fiero jabbed a finger into Clay Taggart's chest. "It must never happen again."

Cuchillo Negro saw White Apache tense and noted that White Apache's right hand was very close to a pistol. Fiero had a thumb on the hammer of his rifle. Another harsh word or gesture by either party might be enough to set them at each other's throats. "I have words to share," he spoke up.

Fiero scowled. "This does not concern you, Black Knife."

"It concerns us all," Cuchillo Negro said. "Or did we not all agree Lickoyee-shis-inday was to be our leader?"

"Lead us, yes. We did not agree to let him treat us as the white-eyes treat one another," Fiero declared. "We did not agree that he can make us do that which we do not want to do."

Delgadito, who had been uncommonly quiet for quite some time, ventured to say, "You make a mistake, Fiero." It had been his idea to have White Apache serve as leader, which at the time had seemed to be a brilliant ploy. Because following the slaughter of the band by the scalp hunters, no one would look to him for leadership any more. He was bad medicine, everyone had claimed. He would never lead again.

The situation had been intolerable. Delgadito had always been a leader, and he would never accept being less. So he had conspired to go on controlling affairs through his unwitting dupe, White Apache.

Never in a thousand winters would Delgadito have imagined the result. It never occurred to him that White Apache might prove worthy, or that most of the band would follow the white man blindly, no questions asked. White Apache had earned the role he, Delgadito, once cherished, and in his private moments he gnashed his teeth at the bitter injustice of it all.

Yet as much as Delgadito detested the usurper, he also had the presence of mind to admit that Cuchillo Negro was right about Lickoyee-shis-inday being the key to the Chiricahuas regaining their cherished freedom. So he spoke in the white man's defense. "It was I who first thought to have White Apache be our leader. Some of you hated the idea. You were one of them, Fiero. And since I knew you would make trouble for him every chance you could, I asked each of you to give your word that you would do as he wanted at all times. We were not to be his equals, but his followers. You accepted."

"Maybe so," Fiero reluctantly said, "but I do not like for him to tell us what to do all the time."

"When does he, except when a life is at stake?" Delgadito countered. "He always asks our opinion before he makes up his mind about anything. He has earned our respect by treating us with respect. We do not lessen ourselves by doing as he wants. Rather is the whole band made strong and fierce."

Ponce could not resist adding his thoughts. "Look at how well we have done since he took over. We have taken more plunder than anyone since Cochise. Our raids are the talk of the whole tribe. It will not be long before many more warriors flock to join us. All due to White Apache."

Fiero felt betrayed. There wasn't a shred of sympathy on the faces of his fellows. They had sided with Lickoyee-shis-inday against him. To add to his discomfort, now that Delgadito mentioned it, he did recall pledging to follow where White Apache led, and to do whatever White Apache wanted. It had been stupid to make the promise. The prospect of so much plunder had dazzled him into making a fool of himself.

White Apache had followed the talk closely. To soothe the firebrand, he commented, "The last thing I want to do, Fiero, is to offend you. I did what I did not to be your master, but to spare you from harm. Your skills are needed in the long fight ahead of us."

The flattery left Fiero confused. He had anticipated a long, heated debate, not to be praised by the one who had slighted him. "I do not need anyone to watch out for my welfare," he said brusquely. "I am a warrior. I walk my own path and take what comes."

"We all do," White Apache said. "And from this day on, I will try harder to respect the path you walk. If I misjudge and overstep myself, you have only to tell me and I will not push my will on you. As for my offense this day, I am sorry, my friend."

The apology disturbed Fiero more than the flattery. Apaches rarely said they were sorry, in part because they were most diligent to not give offense, and in part because they saw making apologies as a form of weakness.

Back in the days when the Nakai-yes mined for copper at Santa Rita, they had always been apologizing for this or that offense. A drunken Mexican would strike an Apache and the leader of the Mexican would say how sorry it was that it had happened. Or an Apache woman would be abused and the Mexicans would send someone to apologize and offer trinkets as a token of their sincerity. But the Apaches were never fooled. They knew when they were being abused, and they knew weakness when they saw it. It was just one of the reasons they drove the Nakai-yes back into Mexico and never let them mine there again.

Fiero became aware that all the others were staring at him, awaiting his reply. "I accept your words, my brother," he said. "Because you have never spoken with two tongues in all the time I have known you."

Cuchillo Negro let down the hammer of his rifle and turned to go. Right away he saw there were only three women, where there should be five. "Where are the sisters?" he wondered aloud.

Ponce spun. He had been so intent on the dispute that he had not paid any attention to the captives. On seeing his two were gone, simmering fury boiled within him. "Where are they?" he snapped in Spanish at Florencio, Cuchillo Negro's woman.

"They snuck off. I did not see which way."

Not for a second did Ponce believe her, but she wasn't his to slap so he merely grunted and scoured the ground. The pair had left well-defined tracks, pointing eastward, and in a twinkling he was off after them.

White Apache thought of the patrol and raced on the young warrior's heels, saying over a shoulder, "The rest of you keep on going north. We will catch up before you reach the Dragoons." The brush swallowed him.

"There. You heard," Fiero said. "Lickoyee-shis-in-day did it again." He sighed and motioned for Delores to start walking. "Telling others what to do must be as natural for the white-eyes as breathing. It explains why they fight among themselves so much, why there was the great war between the Blue Coats and the Gray Coats. They are like small children who push and shove over which one gets to torture a lizard. They have not learned how to live together like adults."

"There is truth in what you say," Delgadito said. The strange actions of the whites had long been a mystery to him. Perhaps, he mused, Fiero had hit on the solution to the riddle. "Look at what they do when they hear shots. Instead of running to a safe place to spy on those who have fired, they run toward the spot as if they never realize that in doing so they might be shot at. Just as our own children would do if we did not teach them better." He paused. "There is no denying the Americans are brave. But now I see that there is also no denying they stay children all their lives. Why should that be?"

No one had an answer.

Over 100 feet away, the one man who might have had something to say on the subject was speeding through the mesquite at a reckless pace, heedless of the thorns and limbs which scratched him time and again. The tracks told Clay Taggart that the sisters were in full flight toward the plain. They had to be stopped before they stumbled on the patrol.

A score of feet in front of White Apache ran Ponce. He no longer had to rely on the tracks to guide him. The siblings were in sight, linked arm in arm as they fled in frantic haste.

Maria glanced around and spotted him. She said something to Juanita, who ran faster.

Ponce kept them in sight. He heard someone close behind him but he did not look to see who it was. He had eyes only for the women. They had humiliated him, made a fool of him in front of the other warriors. Thinking of the punishment he would inflict made his blood throb in his veins. He rounded a bush and there they were, 60 feet away at the end of a straight stretch of open ground. With his quarry so close, he fairly flew.

The women were about to go around the next bend when Juanita tripped over her own feet, bringing both of them down. Maria scrambled to her knees and shoved her younger sister but Juanita took a single halting stride and then looked back. On spying the Chiricahua, she froze.

"Go!" Maria cried, shoving again, but it was like attempting to push a statue. Refusing to give up, Maria hooked an arm around Juanita's waist and forcibly dragged her off. "Move your legs!" she said. "We can still make it if you do your part."

The appeal got through to Juanita. Nodding dumbly, she ran. She never heard the wraith who swooped down on them, never knew how costly her delay had been until a different arm slammed into the small of her spine and drove her to the ground.

Maria also went down, but where Juanita curled up into a ball and whimpered, she fought, scratching at the warrior's face, trying to blind him so they could get away.

Ponce had to let go of Juanita in order to deal with the tigress. He seized her wrists to hold her arms at bay and was kneed in the thigh. As he tucked his legs to his waist to protect his groin, Maria tried to bite his nose off. She was a whirlwind, driven by dread of losing the life she knew and dread of having to live the life the Apaches had in store for her.

Slowly, thanks to his superior strength, Ponce prevailed. He almost had her pinned when he lost his grip on her right wrist and the next thing he knew, she had his knife in her hand and was raising it to stab him in the chest. He could neither block the blow nor flip aside in time.

As the knife swept down, a bronzed hand seized the woman's arm. White Apache had arrived. He threw himself on top of her, pinning her flat while covering her mouth with his left hand. "The other one," he hissed. "Now!"

For a moment Ponce was angered by the command. Lickoyee-shis-inday was doing exactly as Fiero had claimed. Then he heard a horse nicker, and glancing eastward spotted several American soldiers riding toward them. He flattened on top of Juanita, who lay meekly on her side, petrified by his touch.

White Apache had his hands full trying to keep Maria pinned. She had heard the horse and knew that if she could call out, help would come.

Three troopers were scouring the chaparral. In the lead was a corporal who had risen in the stirrups for a better view. "I tell you, I heard something," he declared. "We're not turning back until we've checked it out."

The voice galvanized Maria into redoubling her efforts. It was all White Apache could do to keep her mouth covered. She nipped at his palm and writhed like a snake. In another few moments she would slip free unless he took drastic action. So he did.

White Apache drew his Bowie knife and jabbed the tip into the soft flesh under Maria's chin. She froze, her face twisted in baffled fury. White Apache watched the soldiers, who hunted around for a couple of minutes but did not come close enough to see them. Eventually, at a nod from the corporal, the trio departed. When they were out of earshot, White Apache lowered the knife and sat up.

Maria Mendez lay quietly, her eyes fiery pools of boiling hatred. She had been foiled for the moment, but White Apache knew that her spirit would never be broken. Sooner or later she would turn on them again.

It was just a matter of time.

Chapter Six

It had been ages since Wes Cody visited Tucson, and if he had his way it would be ages before he did so again. There were already far too many people for his liking and more flocked to the capital of the Territory every day.

Cody strode into The Oriental shortly after noon. Once the saloon had been one of the finest in town, but not any more. Ownerships had changed hands and the new owner was more interested in lining his pockets than in upkeep. As a result the place had gone downhill badly. The mirror behind the bar was cracked in a half-dozen spots, while the counter itself bore many scratches and gouge marks made by knives and broken glass. The floor needed sweeping, the spittoons needed emptying, and many of the tables were as scarred as the bar.

The old scout was surprised that Ren Starky would work there. After giving up the grueling life of a scout, Starky had become a professional gambler and done himself proud. Cody had seen the man win piles of money nights on end. Instead of grungy buckskins, Starky took to wearing a fancy frock coat and a white shirt with frills. Big rings adorned his fingers. He had smoked dollar cigars and sported a gold watch and chain. Nothing but the best would suit him.

A portly man in a dirty apron stood polishing glasses with a rag that needed cleaning more than they did. As bored as a man could be and still be awake, he glanced around as Cody approached. "What'll it be, old-timer?"

Rankled at being treated with such familiarity, the scout said, "My handle is Wes Cody."

In the old days the mere mention of his name had been enough to make folks stand up and take notice, but the barkeep merely yawned. It was obvious he had never heard of Cody, which added to his indignation. That was what came of having so many new faces in town, he reflected. The more people there were, the harder it was to be famous.

"And what can I do for you?"

"My grandson tells me that I can find Ren Starky here." Cody sniffed to show his displeasure with the dive. "I can't rightly believe a high roller like him would step through the door, but for all his faults, my grandson doesn't lie."

The bartender swirled the dirty rag in the dirty glass, then extended a dirty hand toward a hall. "Try the third room down. He don't ordinarily join the living until sunset, but I think I heard him coughing his lungs out a while ago."

"I'm obliged," Cody said stiffly. Lifting his Spencer, he went to the right door and knocked loudly. There was no reply. He tried again, impatient to get the meeting over with and get the hell out of town.

"Who is it?" a rough voice growled.

The voice wasn't Ren's. Cody was set to throttle the bartender if the lazy so-and-so had sent him to the wrong room. "I'm lookin' for a jasper named Ren Starky. Can you tell me where to find him?"

A bed spring creaked. Boots scraped the floor. Then the door swung inward and an overpowering odor almost made Cody back up a step. It was a smell he knew all too well from his many campaigns with the army and from all the hunting he had done; the smell of blood, lots and lots of fresh blood.

Framed in the doorway was a scarecrow of a man whose clothes hung loosely, like extra layers of skin. His face was haggard, his eyes sunken. Stubble dotted his chin. Red dots flecked the skin around his mouth and his shirt. He looked for all the world like a man with one foot in the land of the living and the other in Hell.

"Sorry," Cody began. "That damned fool bartender—" Suddenly he stopped. The man's mouth had creased in a lopsided grin, the same sort of lopsided grin his friend always wore. With a shock that made his gut tighten into a knot, he realized that he was staring at the person he had come to see. "Ren? By God! Is that you?"

"Howdy, Wes," Starky said amiably. "Come on in."

Taking a breath, Cody did. The room was in as bad a shape as its occupant. Discarded clothes littered the floor, the linen had not been changed in a coon's age, and the remains of old meals sat on a small square table in one corner. Oddly enough, there was also a spittoon by the bed.

Starky shuffled to the table, uncapped a whiskey bottle, and took a long swig. Smacking his lips, he chuckled and said, "Hell of a breakfast, don't you reckon? I can remember when I'd have five or six eggs and a dozen strips of bacon. Times do change."

Cody didn't know what to say. In all his years he had seldom been so flabbergasted. Not wishing to be rude to one of the best friends he'd ever had, he blurted, "Timmy said I'd find you here."

Starky took another swallow, swirled the liquor in his mouth, and swallowed hard. "To tell the truth, I didn't think that grandson of yours would come through. I figured he was flapping his gums to hear himself talk." The gambler sat on the edge of the bed, head bowed, quivering as if cold. "Have a seat, pard."

"I'd rather stand," Cody said, unwilling to go any further. He couldn't say why, but standing there in that awful room made the short hairs at the nape of his neck prick. The only other time he had felt that way was the very first time he came on an Indian burial ground, up in Sioux country.

"Suit yourself." Starky capped the bottle and let it drop. Despite his state, his blue eyes still blazed with the intensity of the sun when he wanted them to. "So is it all set? Are we going after the renegades?"

Cody couldn't help himself. He had to ask. "Are you sure you're up to it, Ren? I mean, it's a long ride into the Dragoons. Water and grub are liable to be scarce. And there will probably be a heap of fighting." He paused, astounded that Starky's eyes seemed to blaze brighter. "If you don't mind my sayin' so, you look awful poorly. Have you been to see a sawbones lately?"

To Cody's horror, the gambler tossed back his head and cackled as a man half mad. He almost pinched himself to see if he was having a nightmare instead of being wide awake. This wasn't the Ren Starky he had known. This wasn't the dashing lady's man and fearsome gunfighter who could have carved a score of notches on his pistol if he'd been so inclined. "Ren, what the hell has come over you?"

Starky's laugh stopped short. He nudged the bottle with a toe, then let out a sigh which seemed to issue from the very core of his being. "Consumption," he said softly.

In a flash everything was clear, and Cody wanted to kick himself for not guessing sooner. "Are you sure?" he said. "Sawbones have been known to make mistakes. Maybe it's something else and they only think it's consumption."

The gambler raised his skeletal head. "Take a good look at me, pard. A real good look. You're staring at a dead man. I have a year, maybe two, if I take it easy." He gestured at the room. "A year of this."

"If you go after the renegades in the shape you're in, you won't have even that long," Cody pointed out.

Strangely, Starky grinned.

"I don't know, Ren," Cody said uncertainly. "We've been through a lot together, but I might have to draw the line here for your own sake. If I drag you off into the mountains and those butchers make wolf's meat of you, it will be on my shoulders. I don't know if I want that."

For one so ill, Starky was lightning quick. He came off the bed and grabbed the scout by the shoulders. "You can't say no, Wes! You can't! Not if I'm the friend you've always claimed I am." Starky shook Cody, a note of pleading in his tone. "I've never imposed on our friendship before, but I'm doing so now. I'm asking you, begging you, to take me along. I give you my word that I can hold my own."

Wes Cody hesitated. Common sense told him to de-
cline. He would have, too, if it hadn't been for a flood
of fond memories which washed over him, memories
of the good old days when they had scouted together
and given the Apaches hell from one end of Arizona
to the other.

"Please!"

Cody pried his arms loose. "All right," he said reluctantly. "You can come."

"Equal share, like the kid said?"

"That's the arrangement," Cody confirmed, curious
as to why the money was so all-fired important.

A change came over the gambler. Starky straightened and squared his shoulders, and for a few moments he resembled the flashy rake of old. Stepping
to the headboard, he plucked his pistol from its holster. "I meant what I told you about holding my own,"
he said gravely.

The pistol came alive. It was the same nickel-plated,
ivory-handled Colt Starky always carried, and the
things he could do with that gun were a marvel to
behold. He did them now, twirling the pistol around
and around, forward and back, flipping it high into
the air and catching it behind his back, then border
shifting without missing a beat. He was poetry in motion, as fast and graceful as he had always been. At
length he gave the pistol a reverse flip and slid it
smoothly into the holster.

Starky smiled wistfully and patted the ivory grip. "I
may not be the man I once was, Wes, but I can still
shoot a spider off a fence post at twenty paces. I practice every day." His expression sobered. "I still have a
shred of dignity left."

The knot in Cody's gut hardened. He couldn't understand why the Almighty had seen fit to blow out

the gambler's lamp in so grisly a fashion. Yes, Starky had been a man of many vices and few virtues. But did any man deserve so ghastly a fate?

"I'll spend most of the day buyin' the supplies we'll need," Cody said. "We'll head out at dawn. I aim to pick up Iron Eyes, then head into the Dragoons without the army being the wiser." He had a thought. "Do you need a horse?"

"A week ago I would have said yes," Starky responded, "but I won me a fine stallion in a stud game the other night. All I'll need is jerky and such." He displayed some of the slick charm he had always exuded. "It will be like old times, pard. You, me, and the Injun against a pack of murdering scum. And just think of all the money we'll earn!"

Cody could not stand to breathe the air in the room any longer. Nodding, he stepped to the door. "The money doesn't mean so much to me, Ren. You ought to know that."

"Always the noble soul," Starky commented in earnest. "It must have been all that Bible reading you did."

"I still crack the Good Book now and again," Cody said, "but not as much as I should. My eyes aren't quite what they used to be. I can see things far off but when I try to read, the lines set to wriggling like a nest of snakes."

Starky walked over and pumped the scout's hand. "This means more to me than you'll ever know, Wes. I'll never be able to thank you enough."

"What are old pards for?" Cody said. He held his breath until the door closed behind him. In his mind's eye he kept seeing that spittoon, filled nearly to the brim, and he shuddered as he walked off. He was halfway across the saloon when, on the spur of the moment, he turned and slapped the bar. "Give me a whiskey."

The portly barkeep studied the scout as he poured. "He a friend of yours?"

"What's it to you?" Cody demanded. Girding himself, he downed the whiskey in several swift gulps and smiled as it seared him clear down to his stomach. He almost felt clean again.

"Don't get your dander up, old-timer. I know not to meddle in the affairs of others," the bartender said. "But from the way you looked just now, I'd say you didn't have any notion of how sick he is when you went in there."

"No, I didn't," Cody admitted.

"Well, if he's your friend, you should talk him into doing what the doc wants him to do. About a month ago the two of them were arguing right here where you're standing and I heard every word."

"What was the fuss about?" Cody asked, although he felt it might be better not to know.

"Over whether Starky should go to a health resort up to Glenwood Springs, in Colorado. The doc was saying how it would do wonders for Starky's health and might buy him another year or two, but Starky was having none of it. He said he wasn't about to spend his days sitting in a pool of bubbling water with a bunch of other lungers who had nothing better to do than wait around to die."

That sounded like Ren Starky, all right, Cody mused. "I agree it would likely be for the best, but if you know him half as well as I do, you know that nothin' I say or do would get him to change his mind."

"True," the barkeep said. "Sad, though. He was one of the best, in his time."

Cody paid and hurried out. The brilliant sunshine was like a soothing balm and he stood for a minute letting the warmth soak into him. When he felt like a whole man again, he bent his legs toward the home of his son. He disliked having to leave Lobo there, but the last time he had brought the wolf into the heart of town people had raised a stink. Men had cursed him for a fool, women had turned pale as sheets, and sprouts had screamed in fear. The marshal had shown up and ushered him to the town limits with a stern warning to never disturb the peace again.

Blocks before Cody got to the side street where his son lived, he heard the ruckus. So he ran. It was amazing to see what busybodies town dwellers were. A small crowd had already gathered at the picket fence and was giving his grandson a hard time.

Cody waded into the thick of them, shoving those who were slow to move with the Spencer. Planting his feet, he cradled the rifle and glared at the lot of them. "What's the matter with you folks? You don't have anything better to do than gawk at my pet and pester this boy?"

A tall man with a bristly red beard jabbed a thick finger at him. "Is that beast yours, then? How could you be so addlepated as to bring a wolf into town?"

Cody could have lied. He could have told them Lobo was a mix of wolf and dog and most of them would have bought it. But he never lied, and he never backed down when he was in the right. "It's as tame as any dog," he declared. "You have nothin' to fret about."

Lobo was lying on his side, panting in the heat. He wasn't bothered by the antics of the two-legs since he had learned long ago that they loved to make noise and flap their limbs.

"Tame, you say?" the gent with the red beard said. "There's no taming a wild beast like that."

"Have you ever tried?" Cody asked.

"Of course not."

"Then how the hell would you know?" Cody had abided all of their nonsense he was going to. "Get lost, the bunch of you. You can see for yourselves that he's tied to the fence, so he's not about to stray off."

A woman in a blue bonnet spoke. "What if it should bite through the rope and attack one of us? What would you do then?"

"I'd shoot it, lady."

"You would?"

"Yes, ma'am. For havin' such terrible taste in food."

The crowd slowly dispersed, many muttering and casting sour looks at both the wolf and its owner. Cody's laughter only made them madder.

Tim had been standing near the gate. Coming over, he pushed back his Stetson and said, "Thanks, Grandpa. Those folks were getting mighty riled. In another minute or two I was going to go get the marshal."

"Then it's good I came when I did," Cody said. "I wouldn't put it past one of those puny bantams to take a cane to Lobo if they figured they could get away with it." He spat in disgust. "Mangy coyotes."

Tim glanced at the sleeping wolf. He would never confess as much, but he wouldn't mind if the brute was no longer around. Sometimes when he caught it gazing at him, he'd swear it was sizing him up for its next meal. He didn't care how attached his grandfather was to the beast. It was unnatural for a man and a wolf to live together.

The front door slammed and out stalked an older version of Tim. Frank Cody wore a pressed suit and a derby, and he carried himself as if he had a corn cob shoved up his behind. "Father," he stated harshly, "we must talk."

Wes came through the gate, leaned the Spencer against the fence, and squatted to pet Lobo. "What's got you foamin' at the mouth this time?"

Halting, Frank Cody placed his hands on his hips and nodded at his son. "Timothy, go inside. I want words with your grandfather alone."

"Ahh, Pa," Tim said, disappointed. He loved to hear them go at each other's throats when they were mad. His grandpa had a flair for cursing which was music to his young ears.

"Do as you're told, young man," Frank directed. He followed his son with his eyes, his lips a thin line. The moment Tim disappeared, all the anger pent up in him exploded in three grating words: "How could you?"

Wes knew why his son was mad but he acted innocent just to get his goat. "What did I do?"

"You know damn well what I am referring to," Frank said. "How could you be so thoughtless? You've pulled some harebrained stunts in your time, but dragging my boy off into Apache country to hunt down renegades has to be the most boneheaded thing you've ever done."

Unperturbed, Wes replied, "In the first place, your boy is old enough to do as he damn well pleases. In the second place, it was his idea to go after the White Apache, not mine. And if it will make you feel any better, Ren Starky and Iron Eyes are comin' along. Timothy will be well taken care of."

"Oh, sure. A scout past his prime, a gunfighter who

they say is on his last legs, and an old Indian."

Frank clenched his fists and came close to lashing out. And it was not the first time. They had feuded for years over differences of opinion. Frank believed that his father liked to get his dander up just to get back at him for becoming a bank clerk instead of a scout. "I'll be lucky if I ever see him again."

"If you're so all-fired worried, come along and hold his hand," Wes suggested.

"What good would that do? You know full well I haven't been on a horse or carried a gun in years," Frank said. "And I'm not the issue here. My son is. I want you to tell him that he can't go."

Wes shook his head. "I can't do that. He's his own man."

"He's as green as grass. When has he ever tangled with anyone? An Apache would bed him down without working up a sweat, and you know it. The only reason you're doing this is out of spite."

"Don't flatter yourself, son." Rising, Wes pondered a moment to collect his thoughts. He wanted his feelings to be perfectly clear. "Straight tongue. I won't say no because it's high time the boy stood on his own two feet. No, he's never tangled with anyone, but that's only because you hardly ever let him out of your sight. You've had a tight rein on him since the day he was born and it's time you learned that there comes a time when a father has to let the reins go."

"Experience talking, is it?" Frank said sarcastically.

"Yes, it is. I had to let go when you wanted to go live in town, much as it pained me to do so. I'd of rather cut off a foot than have you turn into a bank clerk, but I respected your right to ruin your life if that was what you wanted to do. Now you have to do the same with Timothy."

"Like hell I do. He's my pride and joy. And thanks to you filling his head with a lot of tall tales about your Indian fighting days, he thinks he can go off and do the same. It's hogwash, pure and simple."

"Boys his age have a hankerin' for adventure, for excitement," the scout said. "It's in the blood. You and I could no more stop him than we could a herd of stampedin' buffalo."

Frank Cody shook with emotion. "I'm warning you, father. If my son goes off and gets himself killed because of you, I never want to see you again. Do I make myself clear?"

Wes frowned. "If that's the way you want it, then that's the way it will have to be. It's your choice, though, not mine. I'll do the best I can to keep Timothy from being harmed. But I can't make any ironclad promises. Injun fightin' is a damned tricky proposition."

"That's your final word on the subject? You won't refuse to take him along?"

"I can't, son. I'm sorry."

"Then damn your soul to Hell," Frank snapped, and pivoted on a heel to storm into the house. He was so mad that he slammed the door and cracked the jamb.

The scout sank down next to Lobo and ran a palm over the wolf's soft fur. "It's enough to make a grown man cry," he said softly. "A body does the best he can all his life. He tries to be a good husband and a better pa, and what thanks does he get? In his twilight years the fruit of his own loins can't stand to have him around. Lord Almighty, sometimes this old world is so messed up it makes a man wonder if all the aggravation is worth the tryin'. Know what I mean?"

Lobo cracked an eye and regarded the two-leg. The soothing drone of the man's voice always pleased him.

"Truth is, old coon," Cody went on, "this looks to be my last hurrah. When this business is over, so's my life. I'll spend the rest of my days in that old chair, waitin' for the sun to set." He rubbed Lobo behind the ears. "That is, provided those renegades don't put windows in my skull first."

Chapter Seven

To celebrate the success of their raid into Mexico, the band carved up a horse and enjoyed a feast. They had reached the remote canyon deep in the Dragoon Mountains without further mishap, and for the first time in many days they could relax and take life easy.

The captives acted as if they were resigned to their fate, even Maria, although White Apache was not fooled for a minute.

Prior to the feast, Cuchillo Negro gave the women a lesson in how to build a wickiup. Delgadito and Ponce lent him a hand, but not Fiero. The firebrand would have no part of it. "Making wickiups is woman's work," he declared when asked to help. "Warriors have more important things to do."

"But these are Nakai-yes," Delgadito pointed out. "They have never built one before. How can they do it right if we do not teach them?"

"You instruct them," Fiero declared. "I will not. I am a man. I kill, I steal, I bring back game. I do not sew. I do not make baskets or blankets. I do not build wickiups."

So the other warriors showed the captives how to trim the slender poles which were used as frames, and how to entwine grass and brush over the poles to form a sturdy structure which could withstand rain and high winds.

Only four had to be built. A fifth already stood near the stream which watered the valley. It had been erected before the band left for Mexico as a dwelling for White Apache and the woman and boy who had befriended him a short time ago.

Marista and Colletto were Pimas. She was an outcast, unjustly banished from her tribe by her husband, the chief. When the pair first came on White Apache in the wilderness, he had been close to death's door. They had tended him. If not for the care they had shown, he would have died.

Much to Clay Taggart's surprise, he had found himself growing fond of the woman. Her beauty, her inner calm, her courage, they all struck a chord deep within him. Much to his surprise, she felt the same way, and her boy had taken a shine to him, as well. For the first time in his life, he had a family of his own to look after.

It was all the more surprising because Clay had once vowed never to care for another woman as long as he lived. His first love, Lilly, had betrayed him, had cast him aside for his bitter enemy, Miles Gillett. It had torn him apart, losing her. He had all but worshipped the ground she walked on, and she had repaid him with the vilest treachery. Small wonder he had made up his mind to have nothing to do with females ever again.

Yet, it happened.

Clay thought of all this while watching the crackling flames lick at the roasting horse meat. He was famished. The tantalizing odor made his mouth water, his stomach growl. To his right sat Marista, to his left the boy.

The Chiricahuas were on the north side of the fire while the captives were on the south side. An awkward silence hung in the air. The women were nervous and it showed.

White Apache knew why. On the long trek up from Mexico only Cuchillo Negro and Florencio had grown close. The other warriors had left the captives alone at night. That was about to change. The new wickiups awaited them. After the feast, Delgadito, Ponce and Fiero would sleep with their women for the first time.

Their anxious faces almost made Clay feel sorry for them. He could well imagine what they were going through. But the band needed to rebuild and could not do so without women. Since the Chiricahua women on the reservation believed Delgadito to be bad medicine and wanted nothing to do with those who rode with him, the warriors had been forced to look elsewhere.

It was not a new practice. Apaches had been stealing women from south of the border for as long as any warrior could remember. Not that there was a shortage of Apache women. Many warriors had more than one wife. No, there were other reasons for the practice.

Foremost among them was the added prestige of the warrior who stole a Mexican woman. It was a credit to their ability to steal and lent them more respect in the eyes of others.

It was also true that sometimes Apache wives put their husbands up to the task. The life of a wife was hard. From dawn until dusk she toiled endlessly, day in and day out. Having another woman around to share the grueling work was to her benefit.

As for the Mexican women themselves, it was a fact that none ever wanted to go back to Mexico. Apache men liked to think it was because of their prowess under the blankets, but Clay knew better.

Mexican women feared that if they went back they would be rudely treated. Although they could hardly be blamed for being taken against their will, they would be tainted for life. People would whisper behind their backs and shun them for having been with the demons.

Also, once a Mexican woman bore a child, she naturally wanted to raise that child where it would be most at home. Half-breeds were looked down on by most Mexicans. Apache men rated themselves superior to breeds, too, but they were not so obvious about it, and gave their offspring the same care and attention they did to the children of their Apache wives.

Finally there was another factor, not often talked about, which Clay felt had a bearing. Even though the two cultures were very unlike one another, there was little difference between the life of a peasant woman of northern Mexico and the life of a typical Apache wife. Both did all the cooking and cleaning and mending. Both worked themselves to the bone for men who would not stoop to share their burdens.

Now, staring at the women across the fire, Clay wondered what was going through their minds. Juanita, as always, appeared terrified. Maria was sullen. Alexandra had her eyes closed, as if she were praying. Delores kept staring at Fiero, who was doing his best to ignore her. Only Florencio was at ease, and she sat off to one side, next to Cuchillo Negro.

Clay leaned close to Marista and said softly so no one could overhear, "I expect there will be some screaming tonight. Maybe we should tote our blankets off into the trees and sleep under the stars."

Marista's luxurious short hair bobbed as she glanced up at the captives. "Maybe that one," she said, pointing at Juanita Mendez. "Not others." A missionary from San Francisco had taught her English several years ago, and while she had a thick accent, she was growing better with practice.

"Why not them?" Clay was curious to know.

"Women know no choice. Not want make warriors mad. Not want die." Marista bent to adjust the haunch so it wouldn't burn. "Delores maybe like to."

"You reckon?" Clay said. He had noticed her fawning over Fiero, much to Fiero's displeasure. The warrior had wanted little to do with her since they arrived. It was almost as if Fiero were mad at her for being there, which made no sense.

"Florencio did," Marista reminded him.

"Right soon after we took them, too," Clay said quietly. "He didn't have to beat her or anything."

Marista's lovely lips curled in an enigmatic smile. "Men be men. Some good, some bad. Woman want good one. Not care anything else."

"Some women, maybe," Clay said, thinking of Lilly. To her, it hadn't mattered that Miles Gillett had a heart as black as an anvil. He was rich, and more than anything else she had craved the finer things life had to offer, the luxuries Clay could never provide.

Soon the meat was done. The warriors pulled their long knives and cut off large chunks, leaving the women to fend for themselves.

White Apache sliced portions for the Pimas. They

ate with their fingers, tearing into the tasty meat with their white teeth.

Fiero finished his piece first and started to rise to get another. Unexpectedly, Delores moved to his side and held out her hand for his knife. He hesitated, scowling, then slapped the hilt into her palm. In moments she had cut off another section and offered it to him.

"Is there anything else I can get you?" she asked in Spanish.

"No."

Smiling coyly, Delores moved back around the fire to take her seat. Her eyes never left the warrior. Everyone noticed but no one dared comment.

Most Chiricahus would have been happy to have a woman who waited on them hand and foot. But not Fiero. He bit into the meat without relish, upset that he was still burdened with her. It had not been his intention to keep her. All along, he had counted on her not being able to endure the torturous journey to the Dragoons. She should be in the belly of a coyote, he told himself, not sitting there making doe eyes at him. It was enough to make him gnash his teeth in frustration. He had half a mind to use the knife again, only this time to slit her throat. He would drag her off and leave her for the scavengers to find.

There was only one problem with doing that. He already had a reputation as being dangerously temperamental. Many Chiricahuas shunned him, afraid he would turn on them over the least little slight. Should he kill Delores after going to so much trouble to steal her, word would spread, and the Chiricahuas on the reservation would want absolutely nothing to do with him. As much as he hated the idea, it was better if he let her live.

Besides which, Fiero knew Delgadito would not like it, and he wanted to avoid upsetting the one man who had always accepted him as he was.

Many of the warriors in Delgadito's band had grumbled openly when Fiero let it be known he wanted to join. Delgadito had refused to listen to them. Chiricahuas must stick together, he had said, and not turn their backs on others of their kind. Their enemies were the white-eyes and the Nakai-yes, not one another. Thanks to Delgadito, the warriors had relented.

Fiero often wished the scalphunters had not caught up with the band. By this time he would have been Delgadito's second in command. And when Delgadito fell, he would be able to take the leader's place. With his own band to command, he could drive the hated whites from Chiricahua soil. His people would no longer be forced to live where they did not want to live, and to till the soil against their will. Everything would be as it had been. They would do as their fathers had done, and their fathers before them. Their days would be devoted to raids and hunting, their nights to their women. They would be true Apaches again, not dirt diggers, like the Maricopas.

Fiero shook his head to dispel his thoughts. It was useless to dream about things as they might have been. He had to deal with the here and now.

Delores still stared at him. Annoyed, Fiero rose, slid the knife into its brown leather sheath, and stalked into the night. He would rather be alone. But hardly had he gone ten steps when footfalls sounded behind him. He turned so quickly that the Nakai-yes drew up short, startled.

"What do you want, woman?"

Delores lowered her chin and licked her thin lips. "To be with you," she answered meekly.

"Why?"

"I am yours now."

The warrior should have been flattered but he wasn't. "Maybe I do not want you."

"You must. You took me from the wagon train."

Fiero did not like being reminded of his mistake. "Why are you not like the other women?" he growled. "Why are you not afraid? Why do you not hate me for bringing you here?"

"I am grateful."

"What?" Fiero said, not sure if his ears were working as they should. The Nakai-yes hated Apaches. They would rather slit their wrists than become a wife to one.

"I am grateful," Delores repeated. "You have given me reason to live again. My sadness is gone."

"Explain." Fiero folded his arms. He could not see her face but there was no doubting her sincerity, which was all the more puzzling. Was it possible, he asked himself, that her mind was not quite right? It would be nice if that were so for then he would have an excuse to get rid of her which the others would accept.

Delores clasped her thin hands at her skinny waist. "I have no husband," she began in a subdued tone. "He died five years ago when he fell from a wagon he was driving and broke his neck." She cleared her throat. "He was drunk at the time. He always drank too much. And when he was not drinking he liked to beat me. Morning, noon, and night he would beat me. I lost track of the number of times he bloodied my mouth and nose."

Fiero did not see what this had to do with him. Few warriors beat their women. They could if they wanted but the practice was frowned on. Any man who had to hit his wife to keep her in line was weak. And, too, Apache women were not timid like the Nakai-yes. Any man who struck one might wind up with a blade sticking from his gut.

Delores continued. "He was a bad man, Jose. But there was nothing I could do. We were man and wife, and the church does not permit divorce. So I suffered for many years, trapped in a life I did not care to live." She wrung her hands. "I will be honest with you, Fiero. I was glad when he died. At the funeral I covered my face with a long black veil not to hide my tears, but to hide my smiles."

Her story filled Fiero with contempt. She had been weak and paid the price for her weakness.

"After Jose died, no man wanted me. I am in my middle years, and much too lean. I am not a pretty young maiden. So I lived alone in a hut on the outskirts of Chihuahua, growing what crops I could and doing what odd jobs I could get in order to live."

"Why do you tell me all this?" Fiero said irritably. She was wasting his time and he wanted her to leave.

"Because you have the right to know. Because you told me to explain." Delores locked her dark eyes on his. "My sister is married to a captain in the army. They move around a lot. Now he is assigned to the post at Janos, and I was on my way to visit them when you and your friends attacked the train."

Fiero gestured impatiently. "None of this tells me why you are grateful."

"I am getting to that," Delores said. "You see, I have missed having a man. As bad as Jose could be, he gave me companionship. I had someone to talk to, someone to listen to, someone to share my life with. Do you have any idea how terrible it is to be alone?"

"No," Fiero replied honestly. From infancy Apache

men were bred to be self-reliant, to hold their own counsel, to be alone, as it were, when in the midst of many others.

"Well, I do. And I hated it." Delores stepped nearer and rested her warm hand on his barrel chest. "I am thankful because out of all the women there, you picked me. You could have taken a younger one, a prettier one, but you chose me. I do not know why, but I am grateful." She touched his chin. "My old life was empty. Now I have a man again. And I will prove myself to be worthy of your interest. I will be the best wife I can be, the best wife you have ever had."

Fiero saw no reason to mention that he had never had a wife, that Chiricahua women feared him too greatly to live in his lodge.

"Please do not be mad at me," Delores said. "I know I am being brazen but I want you to know how I feel. I want you to know that you can trust me. I will never try to stick a knife in your back or poison you. I will be yours for as long as you want me."

All Fiero could do was grunt. He was too bewildered to comment. All along he had been hoping she would perish, but maybe he was being too hasty. It might be nice to have a woman waiting on his every need. She would build wickiups, cook his food, make breech-cloths and shirts. When they traveled, she could carry their possessions. The horses he stole, she could look after. The more he thought about it, the more he liked the idea.

"We will see how you do," Fiero stated. "If you please me, you can stay. If you do not, you must go."

"That is fair."

Fiero pointed at their lodge. "Go in and spread out my blankets. I would sleep now."

"As you wish."

The warrior watched her scurry inside to do his bidding. Shaking his head in disbelief at his change of heart, he strode to the entrance, bent, and went in to put her to another test.

Over by the fire, Clay Taggart smiled to himself. Even the hardest men, it seemed, were clay in the hands of a persistent filly. He cut off another sizeable portion of meat, divided it in half, and gave the spare section to Marista, who in turn shared it with the boy.

Presently Cuchillo Negro and Florencia drifted to their lodge. Delgadito was content to go on eating, but Ponce, who did not have much of an appetite, took it as his cue to do likewise. Rising, he wiped his greasy hands on his thighs and walked over to the sisters.

"Come."

Juanita Mendez whined and hugged her knees. Maria looked up but did not respond or move.

"Did you hear?" the young warrior said. "Come to wickiup. Now."

"I'm not tired," Maria said. She draped her arm across her sibling's shoulders. "Neither is my sister. We want to stay up a while yet. You go on without us."

Ponce was not to be denied. The women had shamed him too many times already. He would not stand for another refusal. So, clamping a hand on the older one's arm, he roughly yanked her erect. Maria resisted, holding fast to Juanita, but she was no match for his finely honed muscles. "Now," Ponce stressed, giving her a shove.

Maria stumbled a few feet, regained her balance, and glared. Her fists cocked, she warned, "If you think we are going to let you have your way with us, you are mistaken. We would rather die, savage!"

Juanita nodded vigorously, her eyes the size of saucers, her teeth chattering as if she were cold. "I would rather die than soil my soul," she declared.

"You will come," Ponce insisted. He grabbed at her shoulder but she suddenly leaped to her feet and bounded into the darkness like a terror stricken fawn. "Stop!" he shouted, in vain. In a twinkling the night enveloped her.

White Apache rose. Since stealing the women had been his idea, he felt obligated to help out. Darting around the fire, he said, "We must catch her before she hurts herself."

More inclined to let the woman go, Ponce ran along anyway. He was tired of having to put up with her antics. Her crying, her whimpering, her curling up into a ball if he looked at her the wrong way, were all the acts of a pampered girl in a woman's body. She was the single most immature woman he had ever come across, and it amazed him that she had lived as long as she had. He should never have agreed to take her along.

The younger Mendez was running in blind panic. She made no attempt to hide, no attempt to even move quietly.

A quarter moon hung in the firmament. Its pale light permitted White Apache to keep the captive in sight. She bore due west. At the stream she stopped, but just for a second or two. Dashing down the shallow bank, she forded the shallow water and sped up the other side.

"Stop!" Clay bellowed. "We will not harm you." He wasted his breath. She glanced at them, her features as pallid as the moon, and fled faster, uttering a bleat like a frightened lamb.

Abruptly, Clay became aware of footsteps pounding behind them. It was Maria Mendez, hard put to keep up. "Go back to the fire," he said.

"No. Juanita is my sister. I want to be there when you catch her. I will not let her be beaten."

"We do not plan to lay a hand on her."

White Apache spoke for himself. For Ponce's part, he was beginning to think that Fiero was right, that women should be treated like horses. But then he remembered his own mother, and how tenderly his father had treated her. Neither ever raised a voice or a hand against the other. That was how he would like his own lodge to be, not filled with constant bickering. He peered ahead, recalling the layout of the valley.

"*Lickoyee-shis-inday!*" Ponce called out.

"What is it?"

"The ravine! The ravine!"

Clay Taggart tensed. It had been a while since last they were there and he had plumb forgotten about the sheer ravine erosion had carved out of the valley floor not far from the stream. The sides were 60 feet high or better and too sheer for a mountain goat to scale. Worse, boulders dotted the bottom.

Raising his voice, he yelled in Spanish, "Juanita! Stop! There is great danger!"

"What danger?" Maria cried. "What are you talking about?"

They all heard the chilling scream. A piercing, wavering note echoed to the heavens, climbing in volume as if the screamer were scaling the stars. At the pinnacle of its power, the scream tapered into a ghastly lingering warble which was punctuated by a dull thud loud enough to be heard dozens of yards away.

Clay Taggart reached the edge of the ravine first. He did not need to climb down to see if Juanita Mendez were still alive. Her grotesquely twisted form lay askew on a boulder in a miserable crumpled heap.

Maria Mendez came to the brink, took one look, and wailed. Sinking to her knees, she pummeled the ground with her fists as tears gushed. "No! No! Not my sister! Please, no!"

Ponce had nothing to say. He was sorry the female had died, but it was not his fault. She had brought the grisly end on herself. He would have treated her decently if only she had behaved.

Somewhere in the forest a coyote answered Maria's wails.

Chapter Eight

It had puzzled Wes Cody greatly when his grandson told him that Iron Eyes lived in a shack near Fort Bowie. The Navajo had always been a proud man and refused to have anything to do with the whites except when serving as a scout. The rest of the time, Iron Eyes had lived with his family off in Navajo country.

And for the warrior to live in a shack was another puzzlement. Navajos liked to live in hogans, a conical type of dwelling peculiar to the tribe, just like the Apaches favored wickiups and the Plains Indians were fond of teepees.

So when Cody finally set eyes on the place the warrior was calling home nowadays, Cody was more than shocked. He told himself that he should have known something was off kilter. He should have expected the worst.

The so-called shack was no more than a lowly hovel, a collection of clapboards and cardboard strung together with chicken wire and a few rusty nails. It wasn't fit for chickens to live in, let along a human being.

Cody couldn't understand why his old friend would stoop to live in such a dump until he drew rein beside a scraggly mule and saw the many empty bottles which littered the ground in front of the crooked, cracked door. "Oh, hell," he said to no one in particular, and dismounted.

Timothy Cody started to do the same but the scout stopped him with a gesture.

"I want to talk to him by my lonesome. Ren and you stay out here and mind the horses." Cody glanced eastward at the serrated ridge which separated the dry valley in which the shack had been built from the high walls of Fort Bowie. "And keep your eyes skinned for boys in blue. If they see the pack horses, they're bound to ask questions. And if they figure out that we're headed into the reservation, they'll confiscate all our supplies and send us packin'."

"Whatever you want, Gramps," Tim said. He had gone to too much effort in getting the whole thing organized to let them be thwarted when he was so close to having his pockets crammed with greenbacks. The thought of all that money made him giddy at times and had given him quite a few sleepless nights.

"Don't you fret, pard," Ren Starky threw in. "I won't let any soldiers make off with our stuff."

Cody wagged a finger. "No gunplay, Ren. Not with the army. They'd hound you from here to eternity. And you're a little too long in the britches to become a wanted man."

The gambler smirked. "Hell, I'm not half as old as you, you mangy coot. And I doubt I'll live for eternity. But I'll sheathe my claws if a patrol happens by. Just don't let me hear you gripe later when we're sitting in

Tucson, twiddling our thumbs."

Cody faced the shack. It was odd, he reflected, that Iron Eye had not come out to greet them. They'd made enough noise, and the warrior had always been able to hear a rock drop from a mile off. Well, close to it, anyways.

The scout stepped to the door and rapped once. There was no answer so he took it on himself to fling the door wide and promptly regretted it. An awful stench struck him, almost as bad as the stink of blood in Starky's room, only this time it was the smell of alcohol and sweat and something worse, something which churned his stomach and made him want to add to the puddles on the bare ground which served as the floor.

"Dear Lord," Cody breathed, and held that breath.

Iron Eyes, once the best Indian scout in the Fifth Cavalry, once a noted Navajo warrior widely respected by all his people, lay on his left side, curled up, mouth agape like that of a fish out of water, spittle dribbling from the corner. Clutched in his hands as if it were the Holy Grail was another empty whiskey bottle.

Cody was careful to leave the door propped wide. Going in, he gripped the Navajo's ankles and dragged the warrior out into the sunlight. Iron Eyes slumbered on, too far gone to notice anything short of the end of the world. Cody stared at him a moment, downcast. "How could you?" he asked softly.

Shaking himself, Cody strode to his horse, took a water skin, and without ceremony upended it above the warrior's face, pouring it right into the Navajo's gaping mouth.

Iron Eyes shot up as if he had been jabbed with a red hot branding iron. He yelped, then sputtered and flailed feebly at the stream. A string of Navajo burst from him, replaced by English a few moments later. "Stop! Stop! You drown me!"

Cody stopped pouring. "That's the general idea, you worthless varmint. Here I come to pay my respects for the first time in years, and what do I find? The great Iron Eyes alkalied to the gills and livin' in a pigsty. Why, for two bits I'd drag you back to your people so they can see what you've made of yourself."

The Navajo was momentarily speechless. His seamed face had a hard, leathery look, and his hair, once long and black, had thinned and turned a light shade of gray. "Cody!" he exclaimed in genuine joy. Dropping the bottle, he rose on unsteady legs. His soiled buckskins were half soaked but he did not appear to notice. "Good friend! My heart is glad! I never thought to see you again!"

The scout beamed and clapped the warrior on the shoulders. "You are a sight for sore eyes," he agreed, and bobbed his head at Timothy. "But didn't my grandson here pay you a visit and tell you about the scheme he cooked up?"

Iron Eyes looked and had to squint. His eyes were not what they had once been, and nowadays the bright glare of the sun gave him problems. He saw the face of the young white man as if it were swimming in golden liquid. "I seem to remember him. But I do not know if it was in a dream or if I was awake."

"The damned liquor," Cody said, kicking the bottle. It skidded into another and both shattered. "How the hell could you stoop so low?"

"I—" Iron Eyes stuttered and stopped. He was too choked up to tell of the years of loneliness following the death of his wife. Nor did he see any need to bring up the war between The People and the Army which had ended in disaster for The People less than ten winters past. He knew that Cody knew, just as he knew the scout had heard about the Long Walk, about the many hundreds who had died when they were forced onto a reservation far to the southeast. Only recently had The People been allowed to return to their homeland. But Iron Eyes could not stand to be there, could not stand to see the scarred land and be reminded day in and day out of the death of the Navajo dream.

Cody saw moisture rim the warrior's eyes and impulsively gave Iron Eyes a hug. He could guess what the warrior was thinking about, and he was upset at himself for rubbing his old friend's nose in it. "I am more sorry than words can say," he declared, feeling all choked up inside. "I tried to help but it didn't do any good."

Iron Eyes stepped back and brushed off a tear. "Look at me. I am a child in an old man's body." He mustered a smile. "I did not know that you tried. I thought all my friends had turned their backs on me."

"Never," Cody said. "When I heard that Carson had been picked to corral your tribe, I offered to parley on behalf of the government. Your people had always treated me square, and it was the least I could do." His lips pinched together. "But that peacock Carson wouldn't listen. His orders didn't call for talk, just action. I was told to mind my own business." He spat in the dust. "Between you and me, I don't think Kit had much choice. The government wanted to make an example of the Navajos and they weren't about to let an old bastard like me stand in their way."

Iron Eyes sighed and gazed out over the bleak terrain. "We have outlived our time, my friend. The world has passed us by."

"Buffalo chips," Cody scoffed. "As long as a person

is alive, they count for somethin'. Don't count yourself out until you've breathed your last." His own gaze strayed to the azure sky. "Even then it's not over. The Good Book says that there's a place up yonder for us after we die."

The Navajo remembered the big book Cody had carried in his saddlebags on their campaigns. "You still believe that this life is not the end?" The scout nodded. "The People, too, believe in another life. I hope they are right." Iron Eyes indicated the shack. "I do not mind admitting that I have grown very tired of this one."

Cody smiled. "Then it's good my grandson came up with his plan when he did. Climb on that mule of yours and let's go earn us a small fortune."

"What are you talking about?"

"You don't recollect the talk you had with Tim?" Cody said. "About going after White Apache? About laying our hands on that ten thousand dollar bounty money?"

The warrior tried to recall but the inside of his mind was like a valley on a foggy day. He could not penetrate very far. Still, the chance to be with his old friend again was not to be missed. And the mention of money reminded him that whiskey cost a lot and he was flat broke. "I will come," he announced, grinning. "It will be like the old days. We will show the renegades why our names were once widely feared. We will show the army and everyone that we are men, not dogs to be cast away when we are no longer of any use."

Timothy Cody chuckled. Everything had worked out just as he had planned, and he could almost feel that money bulging in his pockets. Then he happened to glance at Ren Starky and was disturbed by the severe expression the man wore. "Cheer up, Mr. Starky," he said. "Before too long we'll all be rich."

The gambler pulled his wide-brimmed black hat lower over his eyes and uttered a single, cold laugh. "Before too long, kid, we'll all be dead."

Palacio, the Apache, was mad enough to stab someone. Chief of the Chiricahuas, he was an imposing figure in his lavishly beaded buckskins, beaded knife sheath, and necklace of rare shells. He was made more imposing by his bulk, for he had the distinction of being the only fat Chiricahua on the reservation. While many of his people went hungry daily and had to scrounge like rats to find enough to feed their families, Palacio never knew want. He always had enough to eat, always had enough on hand to keep his big belly full for many sleeps on end.

His secret? Palacio was good at manipulating people. He had manipulated his own into accepting him as leader after the great Cochise passed on. He had manipulated the whites into thinking that his influence among the Chiricahuas was boundless, and that they only needed to ask and he would see their wishes fulfilled.

The white-eyes were grateful for the help since they had so hard a time keeping a tight rein on the Chiricahuas. So grateful that they lavished gifts on Palacio to keep him disposed in their favor. It was the white way, Palacio had early learned, and he milked their false generosity for all it was worth. Did he need food? He had but to say the word. Horses? He could always pick from the finest. Clothes, knives, whatever he wanted, he was allowed to have.

Until this very day.

Few of Palacio's people had ever seen him mad. He always smiled, always treated everyone as if they were long lost relatives. But now he scowled as he rode along on his magnificent white horse toward the wickiup of the warrior he needed to visit. He scowled at all those he passed, scowled at the decrepit dwellings in which they lived, scowled at the baked land which surrounded the village.

It was all their fault, Palacio inwardly raged. His stupid people were to blame for the army refusing to give him so much as a kernel of corn. They were to blame because he was sure some of them knew where to find Delgadito's filthy renegades, yet they refused to share the secret with him. It would serve them right, he fumed, if they all starved to death.

Presently the wickiup Palacio sought appeared. He smoothed his scowl and plastered a sham smile on his face. If Sait-jah suspected the real reason for his visit, the warrior would laugh him to scorn. He must be wily, like the fox. He must be determined, like the badger. And above all, he must lie with a silver tongue.

Drawing rein, Palacio oozed to the ground. He stretched first one ponderous leg, then the other. Long rides often cut off his circulation. His wife claimed it was because he was so fat he could not sit a horse right, a claim she had only made once. A cuff had seen to that.

A shadow filled the entrance. From within uncoiled Sait-jah, his own head rising as high as the stallion's, his features as stern as the land which had spawned him. Bands of sinew rippled on his stomach and arms.

Looking at him, one of the fiercest warriors in the whole tribe, Palacio congratulated himself on having made the right choice. "Greetings, my brother," he began. "It has been too long since last my ears heard words from your lips."

Sait-jah wore a perpetual frown which was accented by a scar on the side of his chin. "To what do I owe this great honor?" he asked, his contempt thick enough to be sliced with a Bowie knife.

Palacio overlooked the insult. "I thought we would smoke and talk."

"We will talk. Here." So saying, Sait-jah sat down right where he stood, flowing as smoothly as a cougar.

The chief paused. He did not like to sit on the ground. It would dirty his buckskins and he had already had to change once that day after he broke out in a sweat in the middle of the morning. Seeing there was no other choice, he carefully lowered his ample posterior and made himself as comfortable as he could. "Now then," he began suavely, "how have you been?"

"What do you care?" Sait-jah retorted. "You have shown no interest in my welfare in the past. Why do so now?"

Feigning a hurt look, Palacio said, "Why do you treat me so harshly? What have I done that you dislike me so? If we do not talk as often as you would like, you must keep in mind that I have many hundreds I must look after. I visit as many of our people as I can but the days are not long enough for me to do all that must be done."

Sait-jah was a rock. If he sympathized, he hid it well.

"I do the best I can, being only one man," Palacio said, and thought he detected the hint of a smirk on the iron warrior's face. Going on quickly, he added, "And I think most of our people would agree that I have done a good job."

Still Sait-jah was silent.

"I have gotten us extra food and clothing from the whites, have I not? I get us permission to hunt when it is needed, and permission to travel off the reservation. It was I who talked the white-eyes into giving old Nana many blankets and food when her husband was trampled. It was I who helped sweet Corn Flower and her children when their man was killed by Comanches." Palacio swelled his chest. "I think even you would agree that I always have the interests of the Chiricahuas at heart."

Sait-jah stirred. "Let us look at your words to see if they are spoken with a straight tongue." He counted off on his fingers as he went on. "You say that you get us food and clothing, but much of it ends up in your own lodge. You get us permission to hunt where once our fathers hunted as they pleased, and we should thank you? You helped Nana, I hear, only after she gave you her husband's horse. As for Corn Flower, she is so sweet that it is said you could not resist a taste even though you have a woman of your own." The warrior's eyes were daggers. "Yes, you are a big help to the Chiricahuas."

This was not going as Palacio had counted on. He knew Sait-jah could be difficult but he had not expected open hostility. Since Sait-jah could not be duped by little lies, he would try another approach. "What about you? Are you willing to help your people?"

"Always."

"Even if doing so puts your life in danger?"

"What is danger to an Apache?"

Palacio pretended to be impressed. "I would expect no less from the mighty Sait-jah. Your reputation is well earned. Who can forget the time you slew seven Mexican soldiers all by yourself? Or that time you led the charge against the whites in Apache Pass? Cochise himself praised your work that day."

"Cochise," Sait-jah repeated. "There was a real leader. He gave his heart and soul so that our people could live. And he did not drown us in words, as some do."

Flattery was proving to be just as useless as lies. Palacio held his temper in check and pondered. Warriors like Sait-jah were so forthright, it disgusted him. They saw everything as either good or bad and wanted nothing to do with the bad. Like children, they were not smart enough to understand that life was more complex, that many compromises had to be made if one was to get by.

"Yes, Cochise was great," Palacio admitted. "He always knew what was best for our tribe. I have tried to do as he did but I am not Cochise."

Sait-jah did not reply. He did not have to. His face was eloquent enough.

"I wish Cochise were here now," Palacio went on while making a mental note to find some way to repay the warrior some day. "He would know what to do about the grave problem we face. I have an idea, but I am not so sure it is the right one."

"What grave problem?" Sait-jah asked suspiciously.

"Delgadito and White Apache."

The warrior regarded the chief as an adult might a foolish child. "Some say Delgadito is a problem because he has not surrendered to the white-eyes. Some say he has done wrong and want him to turn himself over to them." There was a meaningful pause. "Others say that Delgadito and those with him are the last true Chiricahuas. Some wish they could do as he has done, but they do not because they have families."

Palacio was all too aware that many in the tribe felt the same as the renegade. They made his life miserable with their constant troublemaking. "I know how they feel," he said. "Many of us would like to go back to the old days, but that cannot be as long as the white-eyes are in control. And because of your friend Delgadito, our people will suffer."

"How is this?"

Here was the crucial moment. Palacio picked his words slowly. "I have just come from the great stone lodge of the whites, Fort Bowie. I was sent for by the white-hair, Colonel Reynolds. He is very mad. So is the White Father."

A derisive grunt was Sait-jah's response. "What do we care? They are only whites."

"We care when these whites have the power to punish our people for acts done by others," Palacio said testily, beginning to lose his patience.

"Speak plainly."

"All right. I will." Palacio tried to square his shoulders but it was impossible to square two sloping mounds of flesh. "The whites say that unless we tell them where to find Delgadito's band, they will cut our food ration in half." Which was a lie in itself. Colonel Reynolds had said no such thing. The officer had merely warned Palacio to either learn where the White Apache could be found or face the loss of all those wonderful gifts from the White Father.

Sait-jah was still not convinced. He was a credit to his lineage, an Apache who only trusted those who had earned his trust. "Why would they do that when we get barely enough to live on as it is?" He became flinty with outrage. "Delgadito has been raiding for many moons. Why do they want him so badly now?"

"Do not blame your friend," Palacio said. "Blame the mongrel he has taken up with. The whites want Lickoyee-shis-inday, and they will stop at nothing to get their hands on him."

"What does all this have to do with me?"

Palacio nearly laughed. He had the arrogant warrior right where he wanted him. "Your concern for our people is well known to me. So is your long friendship with Delgadito. I thought that on their behalf you would go to him and convince him to turn the mongrel over to Colonel Reyolds."

"I do not know where Delgadito is."

"But you could find him if you wanted. The two of you roamed the mountains together when you were younger. Take as many warriors as you need and go hunt him down."

Sait-jah stared into the distance at the shimmering peaks. "I cannot. I will not betray a friend."

Seizing the advantage, Palacio said, "And no one asks you to. Simply ask him to do what is best for our people."

"And if he refuses? If he will not turn White Apache over?"

"Then you must search your heart for the right thing to do. But remember this. The whites want this Clay Taggart more than they want Delgadito. They would be satisfied with him. They would not cut our rations if we give him to them."

The warrior's forehead furrowed. "Just White Apache? Perhaps that could be done no matter what Delgadito wants. Our people must not suffer any more than they already have."

"You will look for the renegades, then?"

"Yes."

A warm feeling came over Palacio, the same giddy delight he always felt when he bent others to his will. Sait-jah was a man of his word. The warrior would find the renegades, and he would bring White Apache back whether Delgadito wanted him to or not. White

Apache would be handed over to the soldiers at the fort, and Palacio would go on receiving the many fine things which made his life so bearable. All would be as it should be.

"I misjudged you," Sait-jah said. "I thought you only had eyes for yourself, but I see now that you do care for our tribe and want the best for us."

"I understand," Palacio answered in mock humility. "It is sad but true that too few of our people see me as I truly am. That is one of the burdens, I suppose, of being a leader."

Chapter Nine

Marista found her man standing at the lip of the ravine, staring down at the spot where the Mexican woman had met an untimely death. She came up behind him and went to loop her arm in his but he recoiled as if he had been bitten by a snake, then looked at her and grinned. A grin which did not touch his eyes.

"Sorry. I didn't know it was you."

"You be all right, Lickoyee-shis-inday?"

White Man Of The Woods. Once Clay Taggart had been proud of that name. Delgadito had given it to him in honor of how well he had taken to Chiricahua ways. It was all the more special because the Apache word for their own people was Shis-Inday, or Men Of The Woods. Another tribe, long ago, had first called them Apaches, or Enemies, and the name had stuck. In fact, the Shis-Inday had been so flattered, they now used it themselves.

But on this day Clay Taggart's soul was mightily

troubled, and he wondered if he was worthy of the honor. It had been his brainstorm to kidnap women to be wives of the warriors, and because of it a young woman had died. He had witnessed a lot of dying since he hooked up with the Chiricahuas and hardly any had bothered him. This one did, though. It gnawed at his innards. "Yes, I'm fine," he fibbed.

"You be not," Marista said. She would never confess as much since the women of her tribe did not fawn over men as white women were prone to do, but she was worried about him. From the day she first set eyes on him, lying half-dead under the blazing sun, she had sensed something special, a strange quality which drew her to him almost as if they were meant for each other. Never before had she felt this way, not even with her husband, a chief of the Pimas.

Clay Taggart put an arm around her slender shoulders. "I reckon I shouldn't lie to you, should I? Not when you're the only person I know of in this world who gives a damn whether I live or die."

They turned from the precipice and meandered toward the stream. It was a tranquil morning. A cool northwesterly breeze stirred the high grass. Nearby, a pair of gorgeous butterflies fluttered. Over by the wickiups a horse whinnied. And the aroma of roasting deer meat reached them, courtesy of the fire Delores had made. She was cooking what remained of their feast from the night before for her new lord and master.

Marista saw fit to comment to take Clay's mind off his troubles. "Fiero and Delores be like this," she said, entwining two fingers.

"Just like you said they would be," Clay said. "You're a heap better judge of folks than I am. From now on, when I need advice I'll come running to you."

Clay inhaled her earthy scent, felt her smooth skin under his arm. He had never expected to have any feelings for a woman after being betrayed by Lilly, yet here he was, caring for someone most whites would brand as a 'mangy Injun.' If they were to walk along a street in the middle of any town in the Territory, they would draw harsh stares and the sort of comments that made a man burn under the collar.

Was that fair? Was that right? Clay had to admit that it was not. And he also had to admit that once he would have been one of the onlookers who regarded with contempt anyone who would take up with an Indian.

It was peculiar, the way things worked out. Life had a way of shattering all a person's settled notions, of showing those who took on airs that air was all they were full of.

Just then a horse galloped from behind the wickiups and over to where they stood. Ponce had a quiver on his back, a bow slung over his left shoulder. "I go to hunt," he informed them, which explained the bow. Using it would save precious ammunition. And they did not care to draw attention to themselves with gunshots. "Do not expect me soon."

"Ride with Yusn," White Apache said. He wanted to ask how the young warrior's night had gone, how Maria Mendez had acted once they were alone in the wickiup, but he did not. It was none of his business. And it was doubtful anything had happened given her spiteful frame of mind. It made him wonder if Ponce really wanted to hunt or if the warrior was using it as an excuse to get away for a spell.

"Will you keep watch for me, Lickoyee-shis-inday? Will you see that my woman does not run off?"

"Is she in your wickiup?"

Ponce stared at the lodge. "Yes. She crawled under her blankets after we put her sister in the ground and she has not been out from under them since. All night long I could hear her crying. When the sun came up I offered her food and water but she would not take them. She still cries. I can stand it no longer." Giving the sorrel a slap, he trotted south toward the canyon mouth.

In English, Clay mused aloud. "Maybe I should take her back across the border. Maybe it would be better if he got himself another filly."

"No," Marista said.

"Why should he keep her? She's not about to let him touch her, not after what's happened. Odds are, she'll slit his throat one night soon and make off with a horse. I don't want his death on my hands, too."

The Pima came to the shallow ford and hiked the hem of her long skirt. "Woman not run away. Woman stay now. Be content."

Clay shook his head. "You had Delores pegged, but I'm afraid you're wrong this time. Maria wants us all dead. In her eyes, we're to blame for the death of her sister."

"No," Marista insisted. "She blame herself. No more hate Apaches."

"I've lost your trail," Clay said. "I don't rightly see how that could be." He escorted her across and they strolled toward their wickiup. Colletto was out front, practicing with a lance Clay had made for him.

"My boy likes you. He think you new father. Him not know we all be dead soon."

Thoroughly startled, Clay halted and turned her toward him. "What the blazes are you talking about? I

aim to last a good many years yet. What makes you
think I won't?"

"You know," Marista said. She glanced at her son,
her countenance as sad a one as he had ever beheld.
"You know."

Ren Starky was mildly surprised that it took the kid
as long as it did for him to get up the nerve to ask the
question. They were four days out of Fort Bowie,
cresting a mesa, sticking to the high lines as any savvy
owlhoot knew to do, when the clatter of hooves told
him he had company.

"Mr. Starky, do you mind if I ask you something?"
Timothy said. He felt awkward around the gambler,
unsure of himself. It was the same feeling he had
around rattlesnakes and wolves.

"This is a fool's proposition," Starky said.

"What?"

"You were about to ask me why I told you that we'd
all be buzzard bait in a few days. Now I'm telling you.
We're kidding ourselves if we reckon we're any match
for a band of renegade Apaches and that turncoat.
Look at us." Starky jabbed a thumb at each of them
in turn. "An Injun whose sole ambition in life is to
drown himself in firewater, an old scout who hasn't
gone up against an Apache in years, a wet-nosed kid
so green behind the ears he could grow corn there,
and me."

Timothy didn't like being insulted but he was not
about to rile a man some claimed was the deadliest in
Arizona. "I don't rightly think you're being half fair,
Mr. Starky. Iron Eyes hasn't touched a drop since he
joined us. Grandpa may be getting on in years but he's
more spry than most my own age. I don't have much
experience at this sort of thing, I'll admit, but I'm will-

ing to learn. And I'm willing to do as I'm told. That ought to count for something."

Ren Starky idly flicked a speck of dust from his white shirt. The kid was just like everyone else, he mused. Few ever had the grit to admit they were making a mistake even while they were making it. Most went through life believing that every little thing they did was perfectly right to do, and they'd justify their actions in all sorts of ways when challenged. It was just part of the human condition, he supposed. Or the human comedy, as he liked to call it. "What about me, kid? You forgot to justify me."

"Justify?" Timothy repeated, confused. "I don't know what you mean. You don't need any justifying. You're the fastest gunman in the Territory. Everyone knows that."

"Talk, kid. Saloon gossip which gets told and retold, growing a little bit each time, until the tale is so tall it reaches clear to the clouds."

Timothy thought that an awful strange comment to make but he did not mention as much. "I don't see where the talk about you is all that overblown. You are almighty fast with a pistol. Folks have seen you when you practice. A lucky few have seen you in a gunfight. Hell, Mr. Starky, I feel safe having you along. If you had refused to come, I'd probably have changed my mind about the whole thing."

Starky glanced at the kid and felt an odd stirring in his chest when he saw that the other was sincere. Peeved, he said, "You missed the whole point. We were talking about why all of us are going to die. About why I'm going to die."

"A man like you? I don't see how."

As if to refute the statement, a racking spasm struck the gambler, doubling him over in the saddle. He quickly fished a handkerchief from a pocket and pressed it to his mouth as he coughed violently for over a minute. The fit passed. Starky straightened, his face the color of flour, his mouth a grim gray line. "Maybe you see now, kid," he rasped.

Timothy only had eyes for the handkerchief, for the bright red stain which covered a third of it. Not really watching his words, he said, "No, I still don't. You're Ren Starky, the best damn shot in Arizona. You shouldn't be talking like you are. Why, if I didn't know better, I'd say that you want to die."

Starky swung around so sharply that Timothy Cody drew back, afraid he had overstepped himself. The gambler's eyes blazed, but not with anger or hatred. He peered intently while Timothy squirmed and looked as if he wished he were somewhere else.

" 'Want' isn't the word I'd use," Starky said, and let the matter drop. The kid had been too close to the truth for comfort.

Just then a gray object dashed past their horses. Timothy's shied. Firming his grip on the reins, he stared at the loping wolf and used it as an excuse to vent his jumbled feelings. "That damned animal! I wish to hell Grandpa never brought it along."

"Be glad he did."

"How's that?"

Starky folded the handkerchief and slid it back into his pocket. "That old wolf has saved your grandfather's hide, and mine, more times than you have fingers. Once, a day out from Ewell's Station, a band tried to sneak up on us about sunrise. We were careless. Both of us were sleeping at the same time. If not for Lobo catching their scent when they were still a stone's throw off, they would have slit our throats while we slept. Either that, or taken us alive to torture. Apaches can be real creative when it comes to inflicting pain."

Timothy looked on the beast in a whole new light.

"Lobo can smell Apaches from a long ways off," the gambler warmed to his subject. "Half a mile or better if the wind is just right. His nose gives us an edge we wouldn't have otherwise. And we need it. Apaches can smell almost as good as a dog can."

"You're joshing."

"Ask Wes or Iron Eyes if you don't believe me," Starky said gruffly. "Never forget that Apaches live in the wild all their lives. They learn to read scents we'd never notice. Take a sweaty horse. You and I could smell one from eight or ten feet away. An Apache could smell the same animal from fifty or sixty feet off. I should know. I did my share of scouting before I took to gambling."

"Grandpa says you were a good one, too. Why did you give it up to make your living at cards?"

Starky gave a short, dry laugh. "I got tired of looking over my shoulder all the time, of always sleeping on the ground, of cold camps and cold meals. I wanted to be able to go through a day without worrying about whether I'd be alive to greet the next one." He laughed again.

Suddenly, ahead of them, Wes Cody raised a hand and halted. Beyond him, the Navajo had stopped and was pointing to the southwest.

A plume of dust marked the passage of a large group of riders. Starky studied them, glad their own party was screened by scrub trees.

"Indians, you reckon?" Tim asked breathlessly, agog at the likelihood of actually going up against a band of hostiles.

The gambler shook his head. "You can put your tongue back in your mouth. Apaches ride in clusters, kid. See how those are strung out in a column? They're soldiers, a patrol out of Fort Bowie. We're lucky they're going in the other direction. If they spotted us this deep into the reservation, they'd haul us back to the post and have us put up on charges. They don't want anyone stirring the Chiricahuas up."

After the troopers disappeared in the haze, Iron Eyes motioned and they rode on.

Tim had been mulling over Starky's comment. "If the government doesn't want anyone riling the Chiricahuas, why'd they go and offer such a big bounty for the White Apache? They must have known that much money would be hard to resist."

"That's the government for you. Coming up with half-baked notions is what they do best." Starky, out of habit, rested his right hand on his Colt. "They likely figured that since Taggart spends so much time off the reservation, the bounty hunters would be nice and polite and not cross over the line."

"But that's plain dumb. Who would ever think such a thing?"

Starky cocked an eyebrow. "I take it you've never heard of politicians?"

For the better part of the afternoon they forged on, never riding in the open if they could help it, never riding fast enough to raise dust. Their mounts and the two pack horses plodded along in the blistering heat, heads low, tails swishing at flies.

At one point Ren Starky took a gold pocket watch from his vest and checked the time. "Five o'clock," he announced. "Another couple of hours and we'll be stopping for the night. It's a good thing, too." Arching his back, he pressed a hand to his spine. "When a man sits on his backside to make a living, it ruins his body in no time."

The end of the mesa was in sight. Iron Eyes, who held the new Winchester Cody had given him as if it were the greatest treasure ever bestowed, wheeled his mule and rode back almost to where the gambler and the kid were. The warrior's dark eyes roved over the mesa, then out over the bluff to the flatland far below.

Wes Cody joined them. "Something wrong, pard?"

"Yes," the Navajo said.

"Mind sharin' with the rest of us?"

Iron Eyes did not want to seem foolish in their eyes, but he could not ignore it any longer. "I have a bad feeling," he said. "A very bad feeling."

Young Tim swiveled to survey the expanse below. "What kind of feeling? What does it mean?" he asked anxiously.

"It mean trouble comes, much trouble."

"What kind of trouble?" Tim pressed him.

"Apaches."

Palacio had been right about one thing. Few Chiricahuas knew the mountains as well as the renowned warrior Sait-jah. He had roamed the Chiricahua Mountains and the Dragoon Mountains from one end to the other. Every spring, every stream, every valley and ravine and gorge were indelibly imprinted on his memory. Much as a white man went to great pains to memorize passages from favorite books, Apaches memorized landmarks and the flow of terrain. Sait-jah had one of the best memories of them all.

He had given the problem much thought since the chief's departure, reliving the wandering done with

Delgadito when they were younger. They had explored every nook and cranny, their boundless curiosity taking them far afield in search of new sights to see, new adventures to thrill them.

Once, they had been like brothers. Sait-jah, in fact, had been the one who let Delgadito know that his cousin was ready to take a husband well before the news became common knowledge. It had given Delgadito an advantage in the courtship ritual. On the night of the maiden dance, when all the virgins had danced in his cousin's honor, he had seen the hunger in his friend's eyes. Not long after she had accepted Delgadito by leading his horse to water, and their union had prospered until Delgadito turned renegade.

Sait-jah could still recall every word said on that fateful night when Delgadito asked him to go with the large band Delgadito was leading down into the land of the Nakai-yes.

"Amarillo is going," Delgadito had said, trying to impress him with the name of a highly respected member of their tribe. "So is Cuchillo Negro and El Chico."

"All good men," Sait-jah had said. "But are they wise men? Is it wise to break up our people this way when our only strength is in our numbers?"

Delgadito had been silent a while. "I wish there were another way but there is not. And I cannot live under the yoke of the white-eyes any longer. They hem us in as if we were cattle, telling us where we can and can't go. They refuse to let us hunt as much as we would like. They refuse to let us go on raids, even south of the border. They have set themselves up as our masters. I, for one, will not be their slave."

"Your pride is strong," Sait-jah had said. "Mine

must be also, because I would like to go with you.
But it is better for our people if the tribe is whole."

Sait-jah remembered the argument which had en-
sued, remembered the sorrow in his friend's eyes
when Delgadito realized there would be no changing his mind. They had parted on good terms, and
it had saddened Sait-jah greatly to later learn that
the band had been wiped out by scalphunters. His
dear cousin had been mutilated, her hair sold to of-
ficials in Sonora. That was no fit fate for a Chiricahua.

A faint scrape on the rocks ahead cut short Sait-
jah's reflection. He glanced up to see Mano Rojo running to intercept him.

Since sunrise Sait-jah had been leading his party of
six stalwart warriors at a brisk dogtrot to the northwest. The seventh, Mano Rojo, had been sent on
ahead to forewarn them of enemies. So on seeing the
strapping younger man, the iron warrior drew up
short to await him.

"Report," Sait-jah said.

"Tracks. Very fresh. Made this day, since the sun
was straight overhead," Mano Rojo said in the precise
Apache fashion.

"How many? Which direction?"

"Five shod horses and a mule which is not shod."

"White-eyes!" Sait-jah hissed.

"They do not ride in a file as would soldiers. From
the tracks, it is clear two of the horses carry much
weight."

Pack animals. Sait-jah withdrew within himself to
think. It was against the law of the whites for any of
their kind to enter the reservation. Only those who
were after something they valued highly would be this
far into the homeland of the Chiricahuas. Could it be

pesh-klitso the whites sought? The yellow iron which they cherished more than life itself? Or were these men trappers, poachers after furbearing animals only found in the mountains?

A third possibility dawned on Sait-jah with all the brilliance of the rising sun. "Which direction?" he repeated sternly.

Mano Rojo raised his arm. "The same direction as we go. We could catch them before the sun set if you want. They do not travel very fast."

The same direction? Sait-jah took a few steps and fingered his rifle. "These whites are after Delgadito and those with him," he declared. "They want the money the White Father has put on his head."

"There is one more thing," Mano Rojo mentioned. "They have a wolf with them."

All the warriors looked at him.

"I saw the tracks," Mano Rojo insisted. "You will see them yourselves before too long. It is a large wolf of the kind we rarely find in the mountains any more. It stays close to one of the horses, as if attached to it."

"Or to the rider," Sait-jah corrected him. His giant frame pulsed with excitement and he clenched his huge free hand and shook it at the sky. "Yusn has smiled on us. There is only one white man who calls the wolf his brother. The scout our people knew as Tata has returned to hunt Delgadito as he once hunted Apaches for the American army."

A warrior named Pindah could not help being skeptical. "It has been many winters since the name of Tata was last heard. He must be very old."

"An old panther is just as dangerous as a young panther," Sait-jah reminded him. He noted the position of the sun and came to a swift decision. "Delgadito is my friend. I will not let Tata kill him. We will follow these whites but not let them know we are there. We will watch them closely and learn their habits. And when the time is right, when they are off their guard, we will swoop down on them and kill them all."

Chapter Ten

Two days after Juanita Mendez died in the fall, her sister came out from under the blanket. Or, more accurately, Ponce pulled her out from under it and dragged her from the wickiup.

It was early morning. Dew glistened on the grass. Birds sang in the trees. The sky was as deep blue as the sea.

But Maria Mendez noticed none of this. She had been dozing when the warrior grabbed her, having cried herself to sleep for perhaps the twentieth time since the tragedy. Her outrage at being manhandled knew no bounds.

"Let go of me, you filthy savage! Take your stinking hands off me!" Maria screeched, while twisting and thrashing as if she were a fish caught on a hook.

Ponce had had enough. He had abided her flow of tears for as long as he could. Now he was resolved to see that she stood on her own two feet. The time for weeping was past. Flipping her toward the stream, he barked in Spanish, "Go. Wash yourself."

"I will not!" Maria raged, not moving a muscle. "And you cannot make me."

Ponce was in no frame of mind to tolerate refusal. Grasping her by the hair, he turned and marched toward the stream, dragging her along. She shrieked and clawed at his arm, drawing blood, but she was weak from her ordeal and from lack of food and could not give him much of a fight.

The uproar had brought the others from their wickiups. White Apache looked on and frowned. He was sorely tempted to tell Ponce that they would find a new woman for him, but then he recollected Marista's belief that the young woman would soon stop resisting.

Fiero smirked in smug superiority. At his side, as docile as a tame mustang, stood Delores. Fiero thought it unseemly for Ponce to let his woman disrupt the whole camp. A man who could not control his woman had no right to have one.

Cuchillo Negro only watched briefly. He appreciated the hard time Ponce was having and knew why. He also anticipated more trouble before matters reached a head.

Of them all, it was Delgadito who moved to help. Striding in front of them, he speared a finger at the woman and snapped, "You will behave, Mexican, or you will suffer. Apache women do not talk back to their men the way you do. Apache women do not kick and scream."

Maria was nearly beside herself. "I am not an Apache! I will never be an Apache. I am a Mexican and proud of it!"

"You are a child in a woman's body. You do not know how to conduct yourself." Delgadito sniffed and returned to his wickiup, giving her a last look of disdain as he went in.

Maria twisted to glare at all of them. "I hate you!" she cried. "I pray that God destroys each and every one of you for what you have done! You are monsters! Devils! You deserve the fires of Hell!"

"Enough," Ponce said. Holding fast with both hands, he hauled her to the bank. She tried to shatter his knees but he sidestepped her blows with ease. At the water's edge he stooped, forked an arm under her back, and catapulted her over the edge.

Maria Mendez landed with a loud splash on her stomach. Sputtering and cursing, she rose to her knees, soaked from head to toe. Mud clung to her chin and the front of her clothes. "Bastard!" she shouted. "You will die for this outrage!"

As calmly as if he were giving directions to a wayward child, Ponce said, "Wash until you are clean. I will not have that smell in my wickiup."

"I refuse."

Almost regretfully, Ponce waded into the pool, seized her by the shoulders, and shoved her under. She was defiant to the last, pushing and punching. She even tried to bite him but he jerked his hand away, drew it back as if to slap her, gave his arm a shake, and settled for shoving her again.

White Apache had seen enough. Bending, he entered his wickiup and took a seat facing the entrance. Colletto was off gathering wood for their fire. Marista set to preparing coffee the way he had taught her.

"I think I be wrong."

"About Maria? Yes, I would say you were."

"She too filled with hate. Not good. Maybe you be right. Maybe she try hurt warrior."

White Apache propped himself on an elbow and listened to the squawks of the captive. "Then I might as well have a palaver with the Chiricahuas later today. Tomorrow some of us will throw her on a horse and head south. We'll set her free near the closest Mexican settlement."

Marista paused in the act of mixing the brew. "That be smart? She know canyon, know how get here."

Clay sat bolt upright. He had plumb overlooked the fact that Mendez might be able to give their enemies accurate directions on how to reach the sanctuary. He should have blindfolded the women on the trip north. But since he had figured none of them would ever see Mexico again, he hadn't bothered.

"Damn me for being the biggest jackass this side of the Mississippi," Clay grumbled. "When will I learn never to take anything for granted? The man who does is asking to be planted six feet under."

"What you do?"

"I don't know," Clay confessed. Letting Maria go would be too risky. By the same token, so was keeping her around. The only alternative was to kill her and he couldn't bring himself to go that far. Her plight was his doing. "I'm open to any ideas you might have."

Marista had a ready reply. "Only one thing can do. Cut out her tongue."

Shocked, Clay blurted, "But that wouldn't do much good. She could still draw a map or write directions on how to get here."

"Then cut off fingers too. Only way be sure."

"I never knew the Pimas were so bloodthirsty," Clay commented matter-of-factly. Her suggestion was all the more surprising since her tribe devoted itself to raising crops, not scalps. Except when retaliating for a raid, they were as peaceable a people as were found anywhere. "How can you say such things?"

Setting down the pot, Marista came closer and gently placed her hand on his wrist. "Want you be safe, Clay Taggart. Nothing else matter. You have many enemy. You must be smart, smarter than enemy."

"I try my best," Clay said lamely. He was both awed and disturbed by what he saw in her eyes. No one had ever looked at him like that before, not his folks, not Lilly, not anybody. Marista was willing to kill to keep him at her side. If that wasn't genuine love, he didn't know what was. It flattered him and scared him, both at the same time.

"Don't you worry," Clay said. "I intend to stick around a good long while yet." He leaned forward to kiss her but stopped when a small form scooted through the opening.

Colletto dumped the wood, smiled shyly, and sat down facing them.

Outside, the screaming had ceased. Clay moved to the entrance and saw Ponce leading a glum Maria Mendez back from the stream. Her slick hair clung to her neck and shoulders, which drooped in defeat. "I have to remember to go see him about her in a little while," he said to himself.

But the first cup of Marista's delicious coffee led to a second, and the second led to a third. All the while the two of them shared their deepest thoughts and planned for a future they both knew would never come to pass. And before Clay Taggart realized it, he had forgotten all about Ponce and Maria.

It was an oversight he would come to regret.

The warrior known as Pindah was too impatient for his own good. That was the considered opinion of Sait-jah after the younger Chiricahua turned to him for the third time since the sun rose to ask the same question Sait-jah had ignored the previous times.

"How much longer must we slink along after the white-eyes like dogs trailing a village on the move? We should kill them soon and be done with it. There is still Delgadito to deal with."

Sait-jah's answer was laced with frost. "I do not need to be reminded of the reason we are here. As for the Americans and the Navajo, we will wait a while longer yet."

"How much longer?" Pindah pushed.

Some of the others shared glances. Mano Rojo, for one, was surprised that Sait-jah put up with Pindah's constant badgering. While every Apache had the right to question another, it was unseemly for any one of them to be so critical of a warrior of Sait-jah's undeniable ability. If it had been up to him, he would have put Pindah in his place long ago.

Sait-jah had the urge. He did not like having his judgment questioned. Prior to leaving the village, as a precaution in case any of the warriors were inclined to act up, he had made it clear that those who went along would be accountable to him. He did not want a finger to squeeze a trigger at the wrong moment. Nor did he want the wrong words said to Delgadito. Tact and patience were called for, qualities Pindah sorely lacked.

"We are close to the hidden canyon so we must dispose of them soon. Tonight, before the sun sets, we will strike," Sait-jah declared. "Kill all of them except Tata. Him we will question. I must know beyond any doubt that he came to slay Delgadito."

"Why is that important?" another warrior wondered.

"If Tata did, and I kill him, Delgadito will be in my

debt. It then may not be as hard to convince him to hand over White Apache."

Pindah scowled and swatted the empty air. "White Apache! Pah! It is an insult to the Shis-Inday to have a white pig named after our people."

For once Sait-jah was in agreement. Why Delgadito had done it, he would never understand. He had heard through an uncle of Ponce's that Delgadito had not meant for it to be taken seriously, that it had been used in a mocking way to belittle the white-eye. Yet that made no sense whatsoever.

A moment later, higher up the sawtooth divide, Cholo signalled.

Sait-jah bounded up the slope in long leaps none of the other men could match. He flattened below the rim and snaked to the edge, rising just high enough to see the rocky canyon below.

Tata's bunch had stopped for a short while to rest their animals and were now resuming their trek. As usual, the old Navajo led. Tata and the wolf were next. Behind him rode a young one in a white hat which was almost too big for his head. Sait-jah had noticed that the young one hovered around Tata when the whites camped. Tata, in turn, was very fond of the boy. That, and similar facial features, gave Sait-jah cause to suspect the pair were related.

Last in line, taking his turn at leading the pack horses, was a lean man in a black coat. This man was sickly and at times would double over in fits of coughing. Despite his condition, it was the opinion of the Chiricahuas that he was the deadliest of the four. He was always alert, always watching behind the party. And he had a gleaming pistol which they had seen him take out a few times and twirl so fast that the gun was a blur. Up and down, around and around, the man's arm had gone, that pistol spinning the whole time. It had been wondrous to behold.

Talking it over at night, the warriors had agreed to slay the sick man swiftly, before he could use that gleaming pistol.

Now Sait-jah waited until a bend hid Tata's party, then he went over the divide and down to their camp. He saw where Tata and the boy had sat and talked, where the wolf had lain, where the Navajo had squatted to listen. He also saw where the man in black had sat, and there in the dirt were small drops of blood. Kneeling, he was going to touch a drop and taste it, as he often did with the blood of wounded animals he hunted, but something inside stopped him, a tiny voice warning him not to put that blood in his mouth.

Going on, the Chiricahuas spread out, four to the right of the trail, four to the left.

Sait-jah moved at the head of those on the right side. Gliding like a ghost, never making noise, and never exposing himself, he kept the whites in sight.

The sun was past the halfway mark. When it rested on the edge of the world, Sait-jah would give the order to attack. The others could do as they wanted but he was going to kill Tata with his own two hands, eventually. And he would take great pleasure in doing so.

It was the middle of the afternoon when White Apache roused himself from beside Marista. He ran a hand through his tousled black mane, donned his brown hat, and went out.

Colletto was over by the trees, using a small bow. Arrows bristled in a target he had fashioned from an old blanket.

Lately the boy never stopped practicing with weapons. Clay suspected that the Pima youth secretly longed to be like the Apaches, to hold his own as a member of the band. And Marista, oddly enough, did not disapprove. From comments she had made, he gathered that she yearned to cut all her ties to the Pimas, to begin her life all over again. She had taken to being a renegade, heart and soul.

The only warrior outside happened to be Cuchillo Negro, seated cross-legged in front of his wickiup.

Clay ambled over. "Have you seen Ponce? I want to talk to him."

"About his woman?"

Sometimes it seemed to Clay that the warrior could read the workings of his mind as if they were an open book. "Yes. It is best if we take her back to the country of the Nakai-yes. She will never be at home among us."

"Ponce might want to keep her."

"After how she has treated him?" White Apache said in amazement. "He would rather drag her behind his horse until all the skin was flayed from her body."

Cuchillo Negro merely grunted. He had been a young warrior once, and he could remember how his affection for a lovely girl had driven him to do things he would never normally do. Foremost among them had been the afternoon he spent up on a high cliff, pining because he believed another warrior had won the woman's heart. So twisted had been his thoughts that he had seriously considered challenging the warrior to ritual combat.

Women naturally had that effect on men. For the woman of his dreams, a man would make a complete fool of himself. Or tolerate behavior he would never stand for in others.

White Apache walked to Ponce's wickiup. Standing to one side of the opening, he called out. There was no answer, so he tried again, only louder. No one replied, nor was there any hint of movement within.

Hunkering, White Apache scanned the murky interior. It took a few moments for his eyes to adjust. When they did, he spied a dark form lying in the center, covered by blankets. Apparently Maria Mendez still mourned the loss of Juanita. "Miss," he addressed her, "I am looking for Ponce. Can you tell me where he is?"

Clay thought the blankets stirred but he could not be certain. After an interval of silence, he tried again. "Maria, answer me. Where is Ponce?" When she offered no response, he said, "It is to your benefit to answer. That is, if you would like to see Mexico again."

By rights that should have elicited a remark, yet it didn't. Clay shook his head in irritation and started to back away. It would serve her right, he reflected, if he changed his mind. As he rose, a low, wavering groan filled the wickiup.

Instantly Clay ducked low and darted inside. The moan had been too deep and raspy to have issued from the throat of a woman. Grabbing the edge of the blanket, he yanked.

Ponce was flat on his stomach, his arms at his side, a nasty gash on his left temple, a puddle of blood under his cheek. A large welt marked his chin and his left eye was partially swollen.

"Damn," Clay said. Rolling the young warrior over, he proceeded to drag Ponce out into the sunlight.

Cuchillo Negro saw and came on the run. "Did she kill him?"

"No, but she gave him a beating he will not soon forget, and he has lost a lot of blood. Bring the others. Hurry." While the warrior dashed to comply, Clay probed the wounds. The gash was the worst and would leave a scar when it healed. Fortunately the bleeding had dwindled to a trickle.

Soon the three Chiricahuas arrived, Cuchillo Negro carrying a water skin which he handed over.

Fiero, of course, was the first to comment. "I knew it would come to this. He does not know how to handle women. He does not have enough experience with them."

No one brought up the fact that Fiero had even less. White Apache lightly splashed water on the young warrior's face until Ponce stirred and opened his eyes.

"Lie still—" White Apache advised, and was promptly ignored.

"The ish-tia-nay!" Ponce exclaimed in alarm, rising much too rapidly. A wave of agony lanced his skull and before he could catch himself, he clutched at the gash and grimaced. Immediately he composed himself through sheer force of will, but he could not keep from gritting his teeth. His face turned the color of a beet.

"What did she hit you with?" Cuchillo Negro asked.

Ponce had to think a bit. "I do not know," he admitted. "I had just dragged her back from the stream. As we went into the wickiup she clawed my arm and I pushed her down." He rubbed the deep scratch. "I walked past her, and I remember bending to pick up the blankets she had lain under for so long. That is all."

"Where was your rifle?" White Apache asked.

"My rifle? Leaning near the entrance. Why do you—" Ponce said, and stopped angry at himself. "She hit me with it!"

White Apache pointed at the warrior's waist. "That is not all. She also took your pistol and your knife."

To say Ponce was furious would be an understatement. He was absolutely wild when it was discovered she had also taken one of the horses which belonged to him. Rising unsteadily, he was all for starting after her that very minute.

"You are in no shape for a hard ride," White Apache observed. "One of us will stay here with you while the rest of us go after her."

Fiero made a sound like a provoked bull. "Why should we help him do that which he should do alone? She is his captive. I am not going." Pivoting, he walked off, allowing for no dispute.

Ponce was not offended. The woman was to blame. She had shamed him yet again, shamed him for what would be the final time. "I need no one to help me," he announced, and headed around the wickiup to where their small herd of stolen horses grazed. Among them was a chestnut of which he was especially proud. It had formidable endurance and could hold to a trot far longer than most horses, which was why he had not eaten it.

White Apache faced the two remaining Chiricahuas. "We can not let him do this by himself he has lost a great deal of blood. He will need our help."

"Ponce slew his first enemy three winters ago. He is a grown warrior," Delgadito said. "We would upset him if we interfered."

"And how upset would you be if we lost another member of the band?" White Apache countered as he jogged toward his wickiup. He slowed just long enough to poke his head inside and say in English, "Maria Mendez has flown the coop. We aim to light out after her. It shouldn't take long." He glimpsed Marista's encouraging smile, then he ran to the black stallion he favored and swung onto the animal, bareback.

Cuchillo Negro appeared. As he mounted a tall roan, he said, "Delgadito and I agreed that one of us should stay with Fiero to watch the women." He turned the roan to the south, the corners of his mouth tweaked. "He gets along much better with Fiero than I do."

Ponce already had a lead of hundreds of yards and was urging the chestnut to go faster. His throbbing head, his aching jaw, his stinging arm, they all reminded him of his lapse. They were like red-hot blades slicing into his body and he could not shut them out no matter how hard he tried. He had let the woman get the better of him again! For that, she would pay most dearly.

White Apache settled into the rolling gait of the black stallion. He did not goad the animal to catch up. Time enough for that later, when the chestnut tired.

It had been hours since Maria Mendez made good her escape. By now, White Apache calculated, she was five to six miles away. Definitely not much more than that, given the harsh terrain. A check of the sun revealed they would be hard pressed to catch her before nightfall.

Out of the canyon mouth swept Ponce. He passed close to a bush and snatched at the end of a thin limb which broke off in his hand. Flailing it as he would a quirt, he widened his lead.

The afternoon waxed, then waned. Perhaps an hour of daylight was left when White Apache and Cuchillo Negro came to the top of a talus slope and spotted Ponce at the bottom, next to the bay the woman had taken. It was down, its neck and a foreleg both bent at unnatural angles, the white gleam of bone visible on the leg.

Gingerly White Apache worked his way to the bottom, slowing whenever loose rocks and dirt slid out from under the stallion. Talus slopes were notoriously treacherous. To go down one too fast was to invite disaster, as Maria Mendez had learned.

"She is on foot now," Ponce declared when the two men were at his side. "We will have her soon."

Before White Apache or Cuchillo Negro could comment, the statement was punctuated by the crack of gunfire in the distance.

Chapter Eleven

It had been a day and a half since the horses last slaked their thirst. So when Iron Eyes wound into a wide canyon and spotted a glistening patch of water off to the right among high boulders, he went to investigate. Then he signaled the others.

Springs were few and far between deep in the Dragoons. Wes Cody thought he knew them all, and he had picked their route to Lost Canyon so that they never went more than two days without striking water. To find a spring he had not known existed was a pleasant surprise.

Cody stared at the sun, quibbling over it being a little too early to call a halt. There was a good hour of daylight left. But he reminded himself that before noon tomorrow they would reach Lost Canyon. The extra rest would insure they were that much more alert when they went up against the renegades. "We camp here," he declared.

Timothy sighed in relief. He winced as he rode into

the cleared space which fronted the spring and slowly slid from the stirrups. His backside bothered him thanks to several blisters. Even though he was a competent horseman, he'd never had to spend over 12 hours a day, every day for almost a week, in the saddle.

Ren Starky was the last to rein up. He wrapped the lead rope to the pack animals around his saddle horn and crooked a leg to dismount.

They all froze when Lobo unaccountably rose from lapping water, turned, and growled. The hairs at the nape of the wolf's neck rose straight up and his thin black lips curled to reveal his tapered fangs.

"What's got that critter so riled?" Tim asked nervously. An excitable wolf, in his opinion, was just as bad as a hostile. He seemed to recollect his pa telling him that wolves sometimes went berserk, killing everything in sight.

"We might be havin' company comin' to call," Wes said casually while shucking his Spencer from his boot. He fed a round into the chamber and walked to a gap in the boulders.

The serpentine canyon boasted practically no vegetation, not even in the vicinity of the spring. The soil was simply too parched. Boulders littered the canyon floor, which angled upward at a gradual slant.

Nowhere did Cody spot movement, but he had learned the hard way to always rely on the wolf's superior instincts. "Tim, bunch the horses under the overhang. Ren, you stay with him while Iron Eyes and me have us a look-see."

"Keep your eyes skinned, old-timer," the gambler said.

Nodding, Cody stalked toward their back trail. Lobo glued himself to his master's legs, his dark nose twitching. Flanking them came the Navajo, his moccasins making no sound, his face as grim as death.

It was as if the decades had been peeled back, as if the three of them had sloughed off their many years of hard living and bitter experience and were once again young, once again in their prime, once again equal to any occasion. It thrilled Wes Cody, sending a tingle down his spine. Grinning, he glanced at the warrior and Iron Eyes grinned back.

Lobo growled again, lower than before, barely loud enough for them to hear. The wolf knew the distinctive earthy scent of Apaches, knew it well, and that scent was strong in his nostrils. Somewhere out there, somewhere close, were the enemies he had spent a lifetime tracking and slaying, and he longed to sink his teeth into them again.

Cody came close to the trail and crouched behind a boulder. After motioning for Iron Eyes to imitate him, he bent and placed his mouth close to Lobo's ear. "Stay, boy. Stay." Then, drawing back the hammer on his rifle, he bolted toward cover ten feet away.

It was a deliberate gamble. Cody needed to draw the Apaches out, needed to get some idea of how many there were and where they were, and the only way to do that was to draw their fire. They might not shoot. They might want to wait another day or so before they attacked. But he was counting on them being ready to make their move, and he was not disappointed.

Hardly had Cody taken three long strides than a young warrior popped up 40 yards away and banged off two swift shots which spanged off the boulder behind him.

The very instant that the warrior appeared, Iron Eyes trained his Winchester and fired. He had feared that when the moment came, his alcohol-ravaged nerves would betray him. He had dreaded having his hands shake so badly he could not aim. But that was not the case. It was as if he had never tasted a drop of the white man's firewater. His arms were as steady as a rock, his eyes as clear as a high mountain lake. The shot caught the young warrior in the shoulder and dropped him.

Wes Cody gained the next boulder. Where others might have quaked at their close call, he smiled. It was just like the old days, those glorious times he cherished, when he had been young and vital and could hold his own against anyone, anywhere. He hadn't realized until that very moment exactly how much he missed that feeling.

Back at the spring, Timothy Cody drew his pistol, fumbling with it as if it were a hot potato. "What was that?" he blurted when he had the revolver steadied.

"Dying time is here," Ren Starky said. He stood as calmly as if he were on the main street of Tucson, his hands loose at his sides.

"I wish you wouldn't talk like that," Tim complained. "And why don't you pull your gun? The savages could be on us at any second."

"Don't you worry, kid. When the time comes, I'll do my part."

Off among the boulders on the far side of the trail, the iron warrior called Sait-jah inwardly burned with anger. He had given clear orders that no one was to fire until he gave the signal, which he had not intended to do until they were close enough to Tata's party to drop them all with the first volley. But young Pindah had rashly failed to heed him and paid the price. He could only hope the fool was dead.

Holding his rifle close to his chest, Sait-jah worked closer to the whites. He had no choice now. He must press the attack. Counting himself, there were still seven warriors, more than enough to finish off the old white-eye and the others. He must rely on numbers instead of the element of surprise.

Sait-jah spotted the Navajo peeking out, seeking a target. Tucking the Winchester to his shoulder, he leaned to the right, snapped off a shot. The warrior disappeared, and he could not say whether he had scored a hit.

But he had. Iron Eyes was on his knees, biting his lower lip against the pain, a ragged furrow in his left side. The slug had glanced off a rib. He just knew it was broken, and he was bleeding badly, but he was still alive. He could still fight. He saw Cody staring in his direction in concern. Iron Eyes plastered a grin on his face and waved to show he was all right.

Just as he did, the Chiricahuas opened fire. Sait-jah's shot was taken as the signal they had been waiting for, and those warriors with rifles poured round after round into the boulders protecting their foes. It was an old trick. Ricochets could be terribly deadly.

Wes Cody flattened as leaden hornets sought his life. Slugs zinged and whined above him, chewed into the ground around him. But he gave no thought to his own safety. His thoughts were on the horses. A high-pitched squeal confirmed his worst fears.

Both Tim Cody and Ren Starky heard the sickening smack of a heavy slug when it tore into one of the pack horses. The animal squealed and reared, which threw the second pack horse into a panic. They strained at the lead rope and it slipped free of the saddle horn.

"They'll run off!" Tim cried, dismayed at the prospect of losing their supplies. He lunged for the lead rope, but as he did, Ren Starky leaped and bore them both to the ground.

"What the hell?" Tim bellowed, struggling to break loose. The pack horses had turned and were making off up the canyon. "Let me go! I have to stop them!"

"Keep your head down, damn it!" the gunman growled.

Only then did Tim hear the buzz of bullets overhead and the whine of ricocheting lead. Slugs were flying every which way as the Apaches poured round after round into the boulders.

Cody's horse was hit in the neck and staggered. It caught its balance, cut to the right, and was on the verge of fleeing when another shot caught it high in the chest with a loud thud. Just like that the animal's legs buckled and it crashed down, blood flecking its mouth and nostrils.

This was more than the other horses and the mule could take. In concert they fled northward.

"No!" Tim shouted. Losing their supplies was bad enough; losing their mounts would strand them afoot and greatly reduce the odds of any of them leaving the reservation alive. He pushed to his knees and grabbed at dangling reins but was hauled onto his back by the gambler before he could snatch hold.

"Damn it! We're dead without those horses!"

Starky paid the kid no mind. He'd fought more than his share of Apaches. He knew their favorite tactics, and he braced himself for the charge certain to come. His hand fell on his Colt, then just as quickly he removed it. Not until the time came, he told himself. Not if the Apaches were to have half a chance to do what he lacked the courage to do himself.

The rifles fell silent. Wes Cody knew the warriors were reloading. In another minute or two they would close in. He bent low and backed up behind a different boulder. Over on his right, the Navajo had also changed position. They were as set as they would ever be.

Awful tense moments went by. A piercing whoop echoed off the canyon walls. Among the boulders dusky specters appeared, flowing over the ground with effortless ease.

Cody caught a glimpse of a warrior here, another there. He tried to fix a bead but they were moving much too fast and using the cover to full advantage. There was a gap of 12 feet the Apaches must cross to reach the inner cluster of boulders, so he concentrated on that strip.

Another volley thundered. Flame and lead cleaved the air. Apaches burst from concealment, streaking across the gap, firing on the fly.

Cody sighted on a swarthy warrior and stroked the trigger. The man went down, but only into a roll. Limping, the Apache rose and dived and reached a boulder no bigger than a breadbasket behind which he vanished as if swallowed by the earth.

Iron Eyes also tried to blunt the charge. He fired as rapidly as he could work the lever of his rifle and he was gratified to see an Apache spin and fall and not move again. But that was only one out of six or seven and the rest made it across the strip.

The scout and the Navajo retreated, their rifles tucked to their shoulders, their eyes constantly darting from boulder to boulder to boulder. Both knew their reflexes had to be razor sharp. Both knew the end might come at any moment.

Back by the spring, Ren Starky jerked Tim Cody upright. "Stay close, kid, and follow me." He made for the boulders, his shoulders squared, his hands still empty.

"Wait!" Tim bleated, seizing the gambler's wrist.

"Where do you think you're going?"

Without warning Starky struck, smashing a back-hand across Tim's face. The kid tottered and nearly fell into the water.

"Don't ever grab a man's gun arm in the middle of a fight!" Starky growled. "What if we'd been jumped just then?" He wriggled his wrist to relax his tense muscles. "Besides which, you spoiled my concentration."

"I didn't mean any harm," Tim protested, his mind awhirl. How could any man concentrate at such a time? The din of gunfire, the stricken horses, they had all rattled him so severely he was afraid his teeth would commence chattering any second. Before he could explain, he saw a husky shape flit toward them from out of the shadows, a shape which held a glistening knife on high. It sprang straight at the gunman. Tim had time to shout a warning but his vocal chords were paralyzed. He could do no more than gape. Which in itself proved to be enough.

Ren Starky saw the sudden terror blossom in the kid's eyes. In a smooth, flowing motion he whirled and drew. The nickel-plated Colt seemed to appear in his hand as if by magic. One moment the hand was empty, the next it wasn't.

Mano Rojo thought he had the white-eye dead to rights. He could have shot the man in black from hiding but that was not his way. He would much rather kill the white dog with his blade, up close and personal where he could see the life fade from the man's eyes.

But Mano Rojo was not quite close enough to strike when the man in black spun and did a strange thing; holding the pistol steady with one hand, he fanned it with the other. There were three shots, fired so swiftly

hey sounded like one. Mano Rojo heard them clearly,
hough, and felt the searing impact as he was lifted
off his feet and flung back into a boulder. He heard
he crack of his spine and felt his torso going numb
as he slumped to the ground. Unwilling to accept defeat, he tried to rise but his hands lacked their custom-
ary strength. A shadow fell over him. He glanced up
into the molten eyes of the man in black.

"Adios," Ren Starky said, and cored the warrior's
brain. Stepping closer to the boulder for cover, he
flipped the loading gate on the Colt and replaced the
spent cartridges, filling the wheel instead of only putting in five beans as was his habit. He flicked the hinge
shut, pulled the hammer partway back, gave the cyl-
inder a quick spin, then smiled and twirled the Colt
into his holster. "Come on, kid. Your grandfather
needs us."

Timothy Cody nodded blankly. He was unable to
tear his gaze from the brains and gore splattered all
over the boulder. Ever since he first came up with the
brainstorm of killing White Apache for the bounty
money, he had known people were going to die. Fan-
cifully, many times he had imagined the battle which
would take place, and in his version it was always the
renegades who were shot dead. Oh, Iron Eyes or
Starky might be wounded in the fight, but the four of
them would prevail and return to bask in the money
and the fame.

But now, staring at a slick piece of brain as it drib-
bled down the boulder, it occurred to Timothy Cody
that maybe his daydreams had misled him. Maybe he
would be one of those to die. The thought left him
rigid with dread.

"We don't have all damn day."

Starky had paused and was waiting. Tim hastened

over, his palm slick against his Colt, his lungs strain
ing to catch a breath. "Sorry," he said weakly. "I don
know what's come over me."

"I do. Take it from me, kid. You're better off bein
a clerk like your old man."

The gambler adjusted his wide-brimmed hat, face
around, and walked toward the sound of gunfire as
he were out taking a Sunday stroll.

Wes Cody and Iron Eyes were pinned down behin
a pair of waist-high boulders. From three sides with
ering rifle fire poured in. Cody tried to snap off a sho
and lost his hat. Iron Eyes spotted a leg jutting int
the open and fired at it. He missed, but the shot kicke
up dirt so close to the moccasin that the Apach
yanked it from sight.

Onto the scene walked Ren Starky. He stepped righ
out in the open and halted.

The Apaches, puzzled by so bold a move, stoppe
firing. Sait-jah stared at the sickly man in black an
felt admiration well within him. This one had cour
age. And something more, Sait-jah sensed. He wa
gazing at a rarity among men, Indians or whites, a
someone who had no fear of dying.

Sait-jah wanted to kill this one himself. Suddenl
rearing up, he brought his rifle to bear. Yet eve
though among the Chiricahuas his speed was rate
second to none, it was as if he moved in slow motior

Ren Starky exploded into action. His first shot, fror
the hip, clipped a tall warrior in the head. Even as h
fired, he shifted to confront another Apache who ha
the same designs. Twice that deadly Colt boomed an
the Chiricahua toppled, neat red holes in the cente
of his forehead.

The other Apaches joined the fray, as did Wes Cod
and Iron Eyes. The scout leaped up and back-pedale

to the north, providing covering fire as he did. "Skedaddle!" he shouted. "Up the canyon!"

Iron Eyes rose to follow. He saw an Apache and leveled his rifle, but as his finger tightened, something slammed into his sternum. The next thing he knew, he was flat on his back. Blood gushed from his mouth, dampening his throat and chest. He felt a hand grip his. He saw Cody's anxious face above him. Then the sky faded from blue to black and his spirit flew to be with those of his ancestors.

"No!" Cody cried, beside himself at the loss of one of the best friends he'd ever had. In an excess of fury he fired wildly at the surrounding boulders. He did not hit any of the warriors but he did succeed in making them duck down. Which gave him time to gain cover, next to Starky and his grandson. "We lost Iron Eyes," he said numbly, although both of them had seen for themselves.

"We'll lose more," the gunman stated, cooly reloading. "Take the kid and head for the hills while you have the chance. I'll hold them off."

Cody looked at him. Ren had always been levelheaded in a fight but he acted even more so now. There was a peculiar gleam in his eyes, which bothered Cody although he could not rightly say why. "I couldn't do that," he said. "I've already lost one friend. I won't risk losin' another." He looked toward the spring. "Where the blazes are the horses?"

"They all ran off," the gunman revealed.

The air was unexpectedly rent by a shriek of agony. It came from an Apache throat. The warrior went on screaming for over a minute until the sound dwindled to a gurgling whine.

"What caused that, Grandpa?" Timothy asked, aghast.

"Lobo."

Into Tim's mind leaped images of the wolf tearin at the throat of a convulsing Indian. Lobo was on thei side, yet oddly enough he almost felt sorry for th Apache. "How many savages are left?" he wondered.

"We'll know soon enough," Starky said.

In the momentary lull, Cody filled the Spencer' magazine. Once all seven rounds were lined up, h poked his grandson. "Let's get while the gettin' i good."

The old scout and young would-be bounty hunte made off up the canyon while the gambler from Tuc son trailed them. They moved as quietly as they coul but all of them knew it wasn't quietly enough. Unsee eyes were on them. The Apaches knew where the were every second and would strike when they judge the time right.

Tim licked his dry lips. "Once we catch up with th horses, let's make ourselves scarce. I'm all for forget ting about the reward money. It's not worth the risk.

Wes Cody nearly broke stride. "What the hell ha gotten into you, boy? We can't turn back now, no when we're so close, not after losin' Iron Eyes. We se this through to the end, you hear? No matter what."

"But we could die!"

"So? Everybody does, sooner or later." Cod thought he spied an Apache and took immediate ain but the warrior was gone in the blink of an eye. "W set out to corral the White Apache and that's exactl what we're going to do. It's important for a man t finish what he starts."

Timothy couldn't believe what he was hearing. "No if it costs his life," he declared. "Nothing is worth tha kind of sacrifice."

Cody looked at his grandson as if seeing him for th

very first time. "A man's honor is," he responded. "When all is said and done, that's the only thing a man takes with him to the grave, except his faith if he's got any."

The boulders thinned out. Ahead lay a short straight stretch leading to a bend in the canyon walls. Lying halfway to the turn was the pack horse which had been shot. It was still alive, but barely. Nostrils flaring, wheezing noisily, it tried again and again to stand but its legs merely dug grooves in the dirt.

Cody regarded the open stretch warily. "There's no way around. We'll have to chance it and pray for the best." Suiting action to words, he sprinted forward. His grandson was close behind while Ren Starky ran at a slower pace, covering them both.

The scout was almost to the dying animal when he heard footfalls coming toward them from beyond the bend. "More of them!" he guessed, and dropped to one knee, using the horse as a breastwork. "They have us cut off."

"Oh, God!" Tim said, falling flat.

Starky caught up but made no attempt to screen himself. Legs planted wide, he glanced from the boulders to the turn, his thumb on the hammer of his Colt.

"Get down!" Cody advised.

The gunman stayed where he was. "You pick your way, pard. I'll pick mine."

Cody was going to ask what Ren meant by that when a figure raced around the bend. He brought up the Spencer to fire and then saw with a start that the figure wasn't that of another Apache. To his utter astonishment, it was a bedraggled young Mexican woman who appeared to be fleeing for her very life. She confirmed it a second later. On seeing them, she drew up short, then smiled in relief and pointed frantically to her rear while yelling in her native tongue, "Help me, please! Apaches come! White Apache! White Apache!"

Tim's Spanish was rusty. "Who is she?" he demanded. "What did she say?"

Ren Starky's brittle laughter fluttered on the hot breeze. "You must have been born under a lucky star, kid. You don't have to go to him. He's coming to you."

"What are you talking about? Who is?"

"Who else? The White Apache."

Chapter Twelve

"It sounds like a damn war," Clay Taggart muttered to himself as he galloped into the mouth of a high country canyon from the north. Ahead of him rode Ponce. Behind him was Cuchillo Negro. They were following the tracks left by Maria Mendez, who in her haste had not taken any pain to hide her trail.

"There!" the young warrior called out, extending his arm.

The fleeing woman was almost to a bend. She glanced back in stark fear, then sped on around it.

Ponce pounded his legs against his mount and lashed madly with the slender tree branch. He heard the gunfire but hardly gave it a second thought. So intent was he on overtaking the one who had made a fool of him that he swept around the bend without due regard for his personal safety.

Ren Starky heard the horse coming. He was coiled like a rattler when the Apache appeared, a warrior with something long and thin in one hand, a lance perhaps. Ren cut loose with skilled precision, banging off a trio of shots, aiming at the rider's chest.

Right then and there Ponce should have died. But the chestnut, catching wind of the fresh scent of blood, veered to the right as the six-gun cracked. The shots missed by the width of its mane.

Ren Starky twisted, compensating, yet as he did the chestnut slid to a stop in a spray of dust and Ponce threw himself on the far side and clung tight. Ren fired at the warrior's arm just as the horse reared. The slug drilled into the animal's body and it let out with a tormented whinny.

Timothy Cody was thoroughly confused. There were savages behind him, renegades in front of them. From out of nowhere had appeared a Mexican woman pleading for their aid. Dust swirled into the air, nearly blinding him. He wanted out of there. He wanted to be back in Tucson, safe and sound in his father's house. Never again would he criticize his father for leading a boring life. Never again would he pine for adventure and excitement. And as for the money, it wasn't worth the price he might have to pay earning it.

Coughing, Tim pushed onto his knees, then nearly jumped out of his hide when his grandfather's Spencer went off almost in his ear.

Wes Cody had caught sight of several Chiricahuas closing in from the rear. He fired twice to discourage them.

It was then that the White Apache came around the bend. He took in the jumbled tableau at a glance and promptly slanted to the right, hurtling past the chestnut which had slumped onto its knees.

Ponce was on the ground behind it. He caught Lick-oyee-shis-inday's eye, and when White Apache nodded, he leaped, reaching for White Apache's offered arm. On the run, he seized hold, held fast, and was swung onto the back of the stallion. A young white-eye in a hat the size of a basket shot at them but missed by a wide margin.

A knot of boulders offered haven. White Apache sped in among them and reined up, springing off the stallion before it stopped moving. Since Ponce had no weapon, he tossed one of his pistols to the warrior, then shielded himself and took stock of the situation.

As yet, Cuchillo Negro had not appeared, with good reason. The seasoned warrior had been the only one of the three to notice a group of panicked horses milling in a wide cleft in the canyon wall. He reined up as White Apache went around the bend, leaped down, and dashed ahead on foot. He was not about to blunder into the middle of a raging battle.

At the corner, Cuchillo Negro peeked out. He saw three white-eyes firing at boulders, saw the chestnut on the ground and Maria Mendez working the lever of Ponce's rifle. Beyond the white-eyes appeared a Chiricahua with a shoulder wound, a man Cuchillo Negro knew.

Pindah. The slug Iron Eyes had ripped through him had torn the fleshy part of his shoulder. He could still fight, still shoot a rifle. So he had caught up with the whites and bided his time. Now, as warriors on horseback materialized around a bend up ahead, he saw Tata turn to face the newcomers. Without hesitation he rose and planted two slugs in the middle of the old man's back.

Ren Starky caught the motion out of the corner of one eye. Instinctively, he whirled, firing a single shot.

The bullet bored into Pindah's left cheek and blew out the rear of his skull. In reflex he tried to work the lever of his rifle. Dead on his feet, he melted as if made of soft wax.

Tim Cody heard his grandfather groan and saw the scout slump over. "Grandpa!" he screeched, hooking an arm around the older man's shoulders. "Ren! He's hit bad!"

The gambler could see that for himself. Snapping shots right and left to keep their enemies from firing, he clamped a hand on the grandson's arm and shoved him toward a boulder midway between those which concealed their pursuers and those behind which the renegades had taken shelter.

"Move it, damn you!" Ren roared. The woman fell into step beside them and he dropped back, covering as always. He saw a warrior peek around the bend and thumbed off a shot which chipped rock slivers an inch from the warrior's face.

Miraculously, Tim reached cover. The woman and the gunman sank down nearby. He gently set his grandfather on the ground and was horrified to see red spittle flecking the old man's lips. "Oh, no," he whimpered. "Not you, Gramps. This wasn't supposed to happen to you."

A nerve-racking silence descended on the canyon.

White Apache didn't know what to make of it all. As near as he could tell, a party of whites had been embroiled in a running battle with a band of Chiricahuas and Maria had blundered into the middle of the conflict. What the whites and the Chiricahuas were doing so close to his band's sanctuary, he had no idea. But it did not bode well.

Lowering onto his elbows, White Apache crawled to where he could see the boulders protecting the whites. He had a hunch that they were after him. Several times in the past few months bounty hunters had illegally ventured onto the reservation to hunt him down, and so long as the government went on offering so much money for his head there were bound to be more.

Even so, White Apache was unsure whether he should side with the Chiricahuas against them or keep out of the fracas altogether. It was no secret that Palacio, the current leader of the tribe, hated his guts and would give anything to see him dead. He might be sticking his neck out for warriors who would as soon shoot him as look at him.

Ponce wriggled over. "What do you think is going on? Who are those whites? Why are other Chiricahuas here?"

"If I knew the answers I would be a happy man," White Apache answered.

Just then Maria Mendez rose high enough to snap several shots in their direction. Ponce took aim but she ducked before he could fire. His anger flaring, he vowed, "She will pay for all she has done. I swear it."

Not 40 feet away, someone else was just as mad at her. "What the blazes did you do that for?" Tim Cody snapped. "We don't want to draw their fire."

Maria scowled. "White Apache," she emphasized. "You know of him, yes?"

"Who doesn't," Tim replied sullenly, wishing to hell he had never heard the name. There was a tug on his shirt and he glanced down.

Wes Cody knew he was dying. Strangely enough, he felt little pain. But he did feel remorse. Remorse for having been harebrained enough to go along with his grandson's crazy notion. Remorse for having led his two best friends to their deaths. And most of all, remorse for having let a rift form between his son and himself. When all was said and done, life was too precious to spoil it by holding grudges.

"I'm sorry, son," Wes said, forming red bubbles with every word he spoke.

"For what? I'm the one who talked you into this," Tim said. His anxiety mounted and he felt an urge to tear at his hair and shriek at the heavens. Composing himself, he lightly squeezed his grandfather's shoulder. "Now you hush. And don't you fret none. Ren and me will get you out of this, Grandpa. You'll see. You'll be back at your cabin before you know it, on that chair of yours, whittling away just like you used to do."

"Not hardly," the scout croaked. "My time has come, Timothy. I just wish I hadn't been so damned full of myself." A searing spasm in his chest gave him pause. He bit his lip until it passed, then said, "Ren? You there?"

The gambler leaned closer. "Need you ask, pard?"

Wes managed to grin. "It's just like in the old days, isn't it? Except back then we had more brains than to let ourselves get boxed in like this." He chuckled, but it sounded more like a sputtering gasp. "You'd think it would be the other way around." With a supreme effort he lifted a hand and rested it on the gunman's shirt. "I've got one last favor to ask."

Ren stared deep into the eyes of the one man who had always been there for him, who had always treated him with kindness and respect. "You hardly need to bother. I know what you want. And you know that I'll do whatever it takes."

"I never doubted it," Wes said, bobbing his chin once. "You always did do to ride the river with," he added more faintly. His eyelids fluttered.

Tim sensed that the older man was fading fast. Terrified, he gripped his grandfather's shoulders and shook. "Grandpa! You can't die on me! I need you!"

Wes Cody's eyes snapped wide and he gave his grandson the most loving look he had ever given anyone. "Enough, Tim. It's time you stopped actin' so pussy-kitten. Be a man. Hold your head high." He opened his mouth again as if to say more but suddenly stiffened. One final, lingering breath he took, then he said, "Where the blazes did that light come from?" And he was gone.

Timothy Cody threw back his head, tears gushing. "Grandpa! Noooooooooooo!"

Fifteen yards off, White Apache cocked an ear and listened to the tortured cry of despair. "There must only be two of them left," he commented.

"And the woman," Ponce reminded him. She was all he thought of. His head still hurt from her blows, but the pangs were nothing compared to the aching knot of burning rage which flamed in his chest. He would not rest until he paid her back. Cautiously rising until he could see over the top of the boulder, he leveled the pistol Lickoyee-shis-inday had given him and pulled back the hammer.

As if in answer to the warrior's ardent wish, Maria Mendez appeared. She spotted him at the very instant that he spied her. They fired simultaneously.

White Apache saw blood spurt from Ponce's right shoulder as the Chiricahua was jolted backward. A .44-40 had enough shocking power to knock a grown man down, and Ponce was driven to one knee. White Apache reached him before the brash warrior keeled over and went to lower him down slowly.

"I do not need help!" Ponce declared, wrenching free. The movement sparked dizziness so intense he swayed and clutched at a boulder for support. "A Shis-Inday shrugs off scratches like this."

But it was more than a scratch, and it bled copi-

ously. The entry wound, located just under his collar-
bone, was the size of a fingertip, while the exit wound
had to be as big as Clay Taggart's fist.

"You should lie down until we can clean the bullet
hole," Clay said, thinking that without prompt tending
infection might well set in.

"I do not need to rest," Ponce said in contempt. He
tried to stand but his knees were as weak as a newborn
foal's and they gave way. Sagging against the boulder,
he clasped his shoulder and grumbled, "Maybe for a
short time it would be best."

The young warrior was not the only one who had
been hit. Lying on her back, an arm pressed to her
bloody side, Maria Mendez fought back an urge to
howl in anguish. She had dropped the rifle and groped
for it, intending to stand and carry on the fight.

"Oh, no you don't," Ren Starky said, snatching the
Winchester out of her reach. "We're hightailing it
while we still can. I gave Wes my word and I aim to
keep it."

Tim Cody was in virtual shock. He gawked blankly
at his grandfather, unable and unwilling to accept that
the man who had taught him to ride a pony at the age
of seven, the man who had taught him to shoot and
hunt, the man who had in many ways done more for
him than his own father, was gone. "It can't be," he
kept saying over and over. "It can't be."

Ren Starky had no time or inclination to be gentle.
The Chiricahuas had been much too quiet for much
too long and he wouldn't put it past the warriors to be
sneaking up on them at that very moment. "On your
feet, kid," he said, roughly yanking the grandson erect.
"Help the filly."

"What?" Tim said, too dazed to comprehend what
was transpiring around him.

"Help her, damn your hide!" Starky commanded. "Unless you want to end up like Wes."

That got through. Nodding dumbly, Tim stumbled to the woman's side and hoisted her off the ground. He couldn't hold her and the pistol both so he lowered it to his holster, only to have the revolver snatched by the gambler.

"I'll need this more than you will," Starky said somberly. The gun had to be reloaded, then he crept westward toward the opposite canyon wall, a cocked pistol in each hand. By wagging his arm he made it plain that he wanted the other two to get in front of him. Once they were, he backed along in their wake. He saw no sign of their attackers but he was too savvy to believe the band had given up. Someone was watching them. He could practically feel it.

And the gunman was right. White Apache had been circling around to where the whites and Maria were concealed when they abruptly materialized in front of him. Well hidden, he watched them, noting the woman's condition, the terrified youth, the whipcord man in the frock coat.

It had been White Apache's plan to get close enough to disarm them. Only after doing so, and dealing with the other Chiricahuas, could he devote attention to Ponce. But now he had been thwarted. They would see him the moment he showed himself. And given the lethal aspect of the man in black, he'd be gunned down in the blink of an eye. His only recourse was to shoot them first.

White Apache stayed low until they were out of sight, then he shadowed them, waiting for something to distract the gunman. A moment was all it would take. Once the man in black was down, the woman and the boy would be easy pickings.

Preoccupied with the fleeing trio, White Apache hunkered behind a boulder. Suddenly he sensed that someone else was close at hand. Whipping around, he beheld a tall, powerfully built Chiricahua in a breechcloth not five feet away. The warrior had a nasty temple wound and held a Winchester.

Sait-jah still lived. He had revived mere minutes ago, thirsting for the death of the white-eye who had shot him. Dogging their heels, he was surprised to see another Chiricahua he did not immediately recognize come out of nowhere. He was about to whisper a word in greeting when the warrior spun. With a start, Saitjah realized that the man had eyes the color of the sky.

Only one person dressed and acted like an Apache but had the eyes and features of a white man.

"Lickoyee-shis-inday!" Sait-jah snarled, and automatically brought his rifle to bear. Or tried to.

White Apache did not know the tall Chiricahua personally. He bore the warrior no ill will. But there was no mistaking the man's hatred or his desire.

Lunging, White Apache swung his Winchester. The two barrels rang together and the warrior's was deflected before the gun could go off. Reversing his grip, White Apache rammed the stock into the Chiricahua's jaw and the man sagged, stunned but not out, his rifle clattering at his feet. White Apache drew back the Winchester to strike again.

The blow had rattled Sait-jah to his core. But his prowess in combat was legendary among his people for good reason. He was bigger than most and stronger than most, but he also had another trait which had carried him through more fights than any Chiricahua alive; he absolutely refused to give up.

So although Sait-jah was stunned, he was far from beaten. Throwing himself to the left, he evaded White

Apache's next swing and kicked with all his might.

It was like being stomped by a mule. White Apache doubled over, the breath whooshing from his lungs. He lost his grip on his rifle and stabbed a hand at his Colt.

The iron warrior pounced. His brawny arms closed around Lickoyee-shis-inday's chest and tightened, the muscles rippling like bands of steel. Once, not all that long ago, Sait-jah had broken the back of a foe by squeezing until the spine popped. Another time he had grabbed a fiery mustang by the neck and wrestled the animal to the ground. Among his people a saying had sprung up: *The branches of a willow and the arms of Sait-jah. They are both the same.*

White Apache was finding this out the hard way. Expanding his chest and straining until the veins on his neck stood out in bold relief, he attempted to break the giant's grasp. It was like trying to resist slabs of granite.

"You die, white-eye!" Sait-jah hissed, agleam with bloodlust.

The pain was excruciating. White Apache swore he could feel his ribs buckling. Any second he expected to hear them crack like dry twigs. If he did not do something and do it quickly, he would die.

Snapping his head back, White Apache drove his forehead into the tall warrior's nose. Cartilage crunched, but those steely bands continued to constrict. In desperation White Apache butted the warrior again, once in the mouth, once in the jaw. At the same time, he speared a knee into the Chiricahua's groin.

Pinwheeling pinpoints of dazzling light exploded before Sait-jah's eyes. Despite himself, he sagged.

Exerting a herculean effort, White Apache broke free. Scrambling backward, his hand brushed a rifle.

He seized it by the barrel, lurched to his feet, and clubbed the giant on the same side of the head as the bullet wound. The warrior crumpled, but incredibly tried to rise again.

"Stay down, damn you!" White Apache said, and swung again with so much force that the stock shattered.

The giant looked at him and began to raise an arm. Thunderstruck, White Apache simply stood there watching those thick fingers draw closer and closer. Just when they were about to close on his windpipe, his adversary groaned and toppled like a patriarch of the forest.

White Apache cast the broken rifle down and retrieved his own. He had half a mind to finish the warrior off then and there but the shot would alert the whites. Deciding to take care of them first and then return, he gave chase, his legs too unsteady for his liking. Fortunately, he doubted his quarry had gone all that far.

And he was right. 70 feet away, Timothy Cody propelled the Mexican woman along under the watchful eyes of Ren Starky. The gambler had high hopes he could get them in the clear. Then a boulder the size of a freight wagon barred their path and they skirted it to find something much smaller lying in the dirt, its coat matted with its own blood.

"Lobo!" Tim cried, forgetting himself.

The wolf had been cut high on the front shoulder and again low on the left side. The latter was deep enough to expose internal organs.

Lobo could do no more than lift his head and sniff. On verifying that the two-leg with whom he shared his food was not there, he laid back down.

Ren Starky halted. He hated to see the poor animal

suffer. Knowing how attached Wes had been to it, he was inclined to put the creature out of its misery. The shot, however, might attract Apaches. He went to go on by and learned the Apaches were already there.

A pair of swarthy warriors charged from the shadows. The shorter had a thigh wound. Both held rifles. They opened fire in unison, one aiming at the gambler, another at Tim Cody.

Starky reacted on impulse, doing what had to be done without regard for the end result. His thumb stroked the hammer twice even as he sprang in front of the grandson. A branding iron seared his chest. Another lanced his stomach. One of the Chiricahuas dropped but the other was tougher and gamely fired again. Starky banged off three shots of his own and was rewarded with seeing the warrior sprawl forward.

The gunman's legs turned to mush. He collapsed against a boulder, his arms drooping. "Go on, kid," he said. "I'm done in."

Tim couldn't let go of the woman for fear she would wind up flat on her face. He hesitated, torn between dread for his own safety and his feelings for the gambler. "I won't," he said. "You've got to come, too."

Ren Starky smiled wearily. "Wishful thinking. I got what I came for. Now go, or it will all have been in vain."

"I—" Tim began, but did not know what else to say. Brimming with tears, he turned and hastened off, not once looking back.

The pair were still in sight when White Apache strode up to the man in black. He had heard the last exchange. It brought back memories of another time, another life, of a different code by which he had lived. He stared after the escaping couple but did not raise his rifle.

Ren Starky looked up. He was too weak to twitch
finger, let alone use a pistol. Squinting, he said, "Blu
eyes? Well, I'll be damned." He laughed, the laughte
dissolving into a racking cough. Rousing himself, h
grinned and said "Ain't this a hell of a note, Taggart?
Just like that he died. His boots were on and he ha
a smoking pistol in each hand.

Clay Taggart closed the man's eyes. Without dela
he ran back to where the giant had been, only to lear
the warrior was gone. Drops of blood led eastward.

"I can take a hint," Clay said to himself. He woul
find Cuchillo Negro, gather up Ponce, and get out c
there before any more nasty surprises were throw
their way. Then it was back to their secret canyon, t
the new life he had chosen, to live by the new code h
had adopted, the code of the Apache.

For as long as life remained.

Jake McMasters

Follow the action-packed adventures of Clay Taggart, as he fights for revenge against settlers, soldiers, and savages.

#3: Warrior Born. Clay Taggart is used to having enemies, and after a band of bushwhackers try to string him up, it seems that everybody in the Arizona Territory is out for his scalp. But it isn't until the leader of the Apache warriors who saved him turns against Clay that he fears for his life. But no one—not a friend or a foe—will send the White Apache to Boot Hill, and anyone who takes aim at Taggart is signing his own death warrant in blood.

_3613-4 $3.99 US/$4.99 CAN

#4: Quick Killer. Taggart's quest for revenge has made settlers in the Arizona Territory fear and hate him as much as the wretched tribe of Indians who rescued him. But for every enemy Taggart blasts to Boot Hill, another wants to send him to hell. Quick Killer is half Indian, all trouble, and more than a match for the White Apache. If Taggart doesn't kill the S.O.B. quickly, he'll be nothing more than vulture bait.

_3646-0 $3.99 US/$4.99 CAN

WILDERNESS
The epic struggle for survival in America's untamed West.

#17: Trapper's Blood. In the wild Rockies, any man who dares to challenge the brutal land has to act as judge, jury, and executioner against his enemies. And when trappers start turning up dead, their bodies horribly mutilated, Nate and his friends vow to hunt down the merciless killers. Taking the law into their own hands, they soon find that one hasty decision can make them as guilty as the murderers they want to stop.

_3566-9 $3.50 US/$4.50 CAN

#16: Blood Truce. Under constant threat of Indian attack, a handful of white trappers and traders live short, violent lives, painfully aware that their next breath could be their last. So when a deadly dispute between rival Indian tribes explodes into a bloody war, Nate has to make peace between enemies—or he and his young family will be the first to lose their scalps.

_3525-1 $3.50 US/$4.50 CAN

#15: Winterkill. Any greenhorn unlucky enough to get stranded in a wilderness blizzard faces a brutal death. But when Nate takes in a pair of strangers who have lost their way in the snow, his kindness is repaid with vile treachery. If King isn't careful, he and his young family will not live to see another spring.

_3487-5 $3.50 US/$4.50 CAN

LEISURE BOOKS
ATTN: Order Department
276 5th Avenue, New York, NY 10001

Please add $1.50 for shipping and handling for the first book and $.35 for each book thereafter. PA., N.Y.S. and N.Y.C. residents, please add appropriate sales tax. No cash, stamps, or C.O.D.s. All orders shipped within 6 weeks via postal service book rate. Canadian orders require $2.00 extra postage and must be paid in U.S. dollars through a U.S. banking facility.

Name_____
Address_____
City _____ State _____ Zip_____
I have enclosed $_____in payment for the checked book(s).
Payment <u>must</u> accompany all orders.☐ Please send a free catalog.

CHEYENNE

JUDD COLE

Follow the adventures of Touch the Sky as he searches for a world he can call his own!

#3: Renegade Justice. When his adopted white parents fall victim to a gang of ruthless outlaws, Touch the Sky swears to save them—even if it means losing the trust he has risked his life to win from the Cheyenne.
_3385-2 $3.50 US/$4.50 CAN

#4: Vision Quest. While seeking a mystical sign from the Great Spirit, Touch the Sky is relentlessly pursued by his enemies. But the young brave will battle any peril that stands between him and the vision of his destiny.
_3411-5 $3.50 US/$4.50 CAN